COP CORNER

A NOVEL BY

J.J. ZERR

Primix Publishing
11620 Wilshire Blvd
Suite 900, West Wilshire Center, Los Angeles, CA, 90025
www.primixpublishing.com
Phone: 1-800-538-5788

This is a work of fiction. Names, characters, places and incidents either are products of the author's imagination or are used fictitiously. Any resemblance to actual events or locales or persons, living or dead, is entirely coincidental.

Published by Primix Publishing   02/21/2023

ISBN: 978-1-957676-40-1(sc)
ISBN: 978-1-957676-41-8(hc)
ISBN: 978-1-957676-42-5(e)

Library of Congress Control Number: 2023902809

Tip of my Curmudgeonly Old Poop ballcap to:
The Bubbettes and Bubbas of Coffee and Critique.
Another tip of the cap to the editors at Primix.

CONTENTS

CAST OF COP CHARACTERS

COP	Descriptor	Spouse
• Hiram Mudd	• Big Hiram	• Glenda
• Oscar Wexel.	• Sawed-off, pro-Trump • Mr. All in favor	• Karen
• Del Sanford	• Former SEAL	• Eunice
• Ollie Fenstermacher	• Fat pro-Trump	• Molly
• Gregory George Normal	• Notso, GG	• Jolene
• Ted Tapman	• Legion Post bartender	• Sybil

Others	
• Owl Ohlenschlager	• Legion Post Commander
• UTHN Hector	• Up The Hill Neighbor of the Normals
• UTHN Arnold	• Up The Hill Neighbor of the Normals
• Fred Tapman	• VFW bartender and Ted's brother

Me and the Wednesday-lunch-at-the-American-Legion-two-beers-only guys was talking last week. Course, that's what we do. We drink beer, eat, and talk.

It's kind of funny. When that COVID business started in 2020, and me and the One and Only Squeeze got ourselfs sequestered with each other, and she only had me to talk to, things got a mite testy. "Talk to me," she said 111 times a day. At one point, she levied a requirement on me to say 100 words to her, each and every stinkin' day.

Well, poop. Didn't she know if there was something to talk about, I'd a talked about it? But see that's one of the differences between men and wimmen. Now setting aside the notion of kissin' and lickey-face for the moment, men think they have a mouth for eating, drinking beer, breathing, spitting chew into a paper cup, using the tongue in their mouth to lick the flap on the envelope to seal it, biting a dog back if one bites you, holding nails when you got hammerin' to do, holding the reins of Silver when you're a riding into a pack of thievin', killin', rapin' outlaws with a pistol in each hand a blazin' away, holding your teeth whether they be God-given or store- bought, and talkin'.

Now wimmen, they think they have a mouth for talking, for eating and talking, sipping iced tea through a straw and talking, breathing and talking, kissing babies and talking, and talking and talking.

And now, even though COVID things have loosed up some, and the Squeeze is, once again, hobnobbing with her wimmen buds, she still demands her daily dose of words from me. So anyway, back to last week at the Legion, I took a slug from my longneck and told the boys about my 100-words-a-day requirement.

Hiram, sitting across from me with a French fry dripping ketchup on the way to his mouth, stopped the fry in midair. "God Almighty, please don't let my Glenda hear about that. Coupla' nights ago, I was watching a cop show when she plops down on the sofa and starts talking to me. Now we was just about to get the big reveal. You know, seven minutes before the end of the show, when you finally figure out who the guilty bastard is. You just don't want to miss that last seven minutes. But did she realize what she was busting into? She did not. So, I told her, 'Just hang on, Hon. I'll be with you in a minute.'"

Oscar, seated next to me, said, "Didn't work, did it?"

Hiram shook his head.

Then Del, he always sits across from Oscar, piped

in with, "See, what I don't understand is we pay money for TV service. Now, my Eunice is always harping on saving money, not wasting it. So, I figure, in paying my TV bill, I'm hiring people to do talking. So, if I don't listen to the actors and actresses say their words, I've wasted money, right? But does she let me watch my shows? Course not. When Eunice wants to talk, she plops down on her end of the sofa, grabs the remote, clicks off the TV, and says, 'We have to talk.'"

"And do we talk about anything important?" Hiram said. "Like how to end global warming, how to avoid nuclear war with the Russians, or how to stop another COVID attack from the Chinese."

"Fact is," Del said. "I can't even remember what we talked about last night when she did it seven minutes before the end of FBI."

"I can remember what Molly and me talked about," said Ollie. "Vaccination. Same thing we talk about every night."

Ollie sits all the way at the end of our table. He's anti-vax. The rest of us are pro-vax. If everybody got the needle, we could get rid of the stupid masks. Course, Ollie, he's got a heart condition, and his doc give him a pass, so he don't need to get the shot. Least that's what he says. We were suspicious he made that up, but we give him the benefit of the doubt and considered the evidence. Now Ollie used to like his beer. Now, though, he drinks fizzy water. Did his doc put him on the wagon cause of his heart and all? That's one piece a evidence. Molly used to go with

Ollie to the doctor, but cause a COVID, she can't no more. If she'd been with him, we wouldn't think of questioning Ollie's heart condition. There's that. Molly wasn't there.

The rest of us talked about Ollie's heart one day when he wasn't there. We weighed the two bits of flimsy evidence we had. One piece saying, "Guilty as sin." The other, "Innocent as all get-out."

"Occam's Razor," I said.

What the hell's that?" from Norb.

"It's a principle," sez I, "that the simplest explanation is the one to go with."

Norb grinned. "That settles it. He's lying about his heart."

"Now, wait a minute," Hiram said. "Why wouldn't the simplest explanation be that he's telling the truth? When he told about his heart, his pants didn't catch on fire."

"Politicians lie all the time" Del said. "Their pants don't never catch on fire."

Oscar said, "On TV, they're always standing behind a podium, so you can't see their pants smoldering."

I piped in with, "Ollie is vainglorious."

Ollie and his wife Molly both have shoulder-length brown hair. When the sun catches their tresses, it looks like God ladled a dollop of molten gold on their heads, or maybe it's turkey gravy. Anyway, they both color their hair at home and use the same hairdresser. Ollie always reminds me of General George Armstrong Custer with his flowing locks. Course, they depict him as a blond in the movies. Goldilocks. In Ollie's case, he'd have to be Brunettilocks. Which is way too Eye-tallion sounding for a guy whose last name is Fenstermacher. Brownie-locks then.

Brownie-locks is sure proud of his hair. The rest of us at the table don't have much of that. Hair. Hiram has a band of it about two inches wide running around the back of his head, while the top is shiny enough to have been buffed by a shoe-shine rag before he came to the American Legion Hall. The rest of us have a few lonely, wiry scraggles on top. The rest of us can't grow hair anywhere but in our noses and ears. But Brownie-locks, he's sure proud of his hair. Vainglorious as all get-out.

"Vainglorious!" from Norb. "What the hell does that mean?"

"It means he's peacock-proud about his hair," I said.

"Well, why didn't you just say that instead of that vainglorious crap?" Norb said. "Peacock-proud. Same as saying he's a liar. Ollie's doc never give him no pass."

We talked about Ollie some more, and we all agreed. Ollie had lied about his doc giving him a vaccination pass. We also decided we were not going to accuse him of lying. Even with Occam's razor and the deadly sin of pride, there was still a sliver of reasonable doubt that Ollie's pants didn't catch fire because he told the truth. Of course, from then on, we'd be attentive to his words and deeds, looking for him to slip up and give us the incontrovertible evidence.

And here's the other thing. Ollie got the flu shot early every year, and he pinged on us to get ours. When I came down with a dose of shingles in the summer, Ollie pointed a finger at me and said I was stupid. I should have gotten the shingles vaccine like he did. But here we are with the COVID vax, and suddenly, this one, he has to be protected from????

Anyway, this got Del to bring up the big incident in Ferguson, and the "he had his hands up when the cop shot him," thing. Which, it turned out, proved to be false, but of course, the world wide web doesn't do retractions.

"To this day," Del said, "I bet more than half the people in the country—hell, in the whole blinking world—believe he had his hands up when he was shot."

"Well," I said, "we don't believe it, just like we don't believe Ollie's mendacity."

Which got me a frown from Norb. But I pressed on. "Now the cops are the bad guys. Same as we military people were during Nam. When we traveled commercial, we didn't wear our uniforms so we wouldn't get spat at. Now the cops are getting spit on."

"You know what's a crying shame these days?" Oscar said.

Like a fool, I said, "No, I don't."

Oscar looked pleased as all get out that somebody chomped on his baited hook. "Everybody's got a voice these days. On the world-wide web. Get there first and loud and you have established TRUTH ALMIGHTY. We need a place where we can put OUR truth out there."

"Our truth?" I was plumb puzzled. "Why do us Wednesday-lunch-at-the-American-Legion-two-beers-only guys need our truth posted out"—I waved my hand—"there?"

Oscar got this absolutely Messianic look in his eyes. (He probably had a couple of extra beers). "No. Not the lunch bunch. I'm talking a much greater, grander body of folks. I'm talking the National Confederation of Curmudgeonly Old Poops."

It turned out that Oscar, Norb, and Del had been having daily lunch (except for closed-on-Mondays Mondays) at the Legion Hall for the last ten days. And they'd been lamenting what the younger generations were doing with the totally squared-away world our generation had passed on to them.

"We decided," Oscar announced, "that the world was going to hell in a handbasket."

"And it's hell bent for election to get there," Norb said.

"And there's not one dad-burned thing we can do about it," Del added.

Oscar again: "But then we decided there was something we could do. The younger generations consider us to be Curmudgeonly Old Poops. So, we decided the first thing we should do was to just accept that fact. We are indeed Curmudgeonly Old Poops."

Norb again: "That's because of the three things we believe: The world is going to hell; It is hell bent to get there; and There's not one blinkin' thing anybody can do to stop it."

Del again: "But then we decided there is something we can do. We can get OUR truth out there."

"And that's where you come in, Notso," Oscar said.

Now, my God-given name is Gregory George Normal. Can you see how the Notso moniker got stuck on me? Notso is sort of like a pastie. It covers up something you can see with your imagination better than you can with your eyeballs. Now, I hasten to add, the only thing I know about pasties is what I learned during the Great-wardrobe-malfunction Super Bowl halftime show.

"Me?"

"Yep. You're up on this Internet stuff more than the rest of us."

"Right," from Norb. "You published that book last year, and you put up a web site and a Facebook account to pimp it."

"Promote," I said. "I'd have said promote."

"Sure," Oscar said. "That's cause you're vainglorious at times." Hiram snorted a mouthful of beer back into his cup. "And Norb and Del and me, we're the editorial review board, so we'll keep you clear of that kind of claptrap."

"Right," Del said. "This is what we decided. You'll set up a Facebook account and call it Dispatches from COP Corner."

"COP," Oscar said. "Curmudgeonly Old Poop. See?"

"And," Norb said, "you'll post a dispatch ever Thursday. The day after our lunch day. See?"

"This is crazy," I countered. "I could write one dispatch saying we are Curmudgeonly Old Poops, that the world is going to hell, that it's in a hurry to get there, and there's not a thing anybody can do to stop it. What would I say after that?"

"We've thought of everything," Oscar said. "We've got a subject-of-the-week-and-content committee, too. They'll assemble ideas. All you'll have to do is make a silk-purse story out of their sows' ears words. Easy peasy, see?"

Easy peasy! My hairy a— Oh, yeah. There is that other place I still grow hair.

✦✦◆✦◆✦✦

I always leave the post at four. Jeopardy comes on at four-thirty. Never miss that. I always get home by four-fifteen. So, I have time to brush my teeth. Which my One and Only Squeeze insists on for two reasons. One, to get the foul stench of beer out of my mouth. Two, she says brushing my teeth will remind me to leave behind the gutter-trash way I talk with my buds back there at the American Legion Post.

After brushing, I spat out the toothpaste, rinsed, and gargled with Blisterine, I call it. Then I think about leaving my gutter-trash talking ways back there at the Legion. After thinking that, I am powerless before the urge to reply to that thought with: Yes, Dear.

<hr>

The next day, being Thursday, I went back to the Legion Post at lunchtime. Mind you, I didn't say anything to the Squeeze. She believes two beers a week is two too many, but just tolerable. If I'd a asked her about going two days in a row, to drink beer, I'd have been going to hell in a handbasket. She'd have been in an almighty hurry to send me there, and there's not one stinkin', blinkin', bloody thing anybody could do about it.

So, I didn't ask. I learned in the US Navy that it's easier to ask for forgiveness than it is to get permission. Though I will admit to a touch of uneasiness as I drove the old pickup to the Legion. Maybe more than a touch. My butt squirmed in my Depends on the seat, just a thinkin' on what she'd do if she found out. As I turned into the parking lot, I decided: No beer. Not even one. Without beer breath, she could not convict. Sort of like the OJ glove bit. See?

Thinking that buoyed my spirits.

Inside, I was relieved to find Oscar, Norb, and Del at our table. In another way, I was a mite uneasy. If they hadn't been there, I could've departed and left The Dispatches from COP Corner in that dustbin where short-term memory dumps things to be never retrieved again.

But they were there. And Damn the torpedoes. Full speed ahead. I couldn't wait to tell the three of them what I thought about last night before going to sleep.

They looked at me as I scooted back a folding chair. Norb told Del to fetch me a beer.

"No beer," I said. "Make it a fizzy water."

They looked at me again, bepuzzlement writ loud on their faces.

Then Oscar grinned. "The Squeeze. If you ain't got no valor, you best have a boatload of discretion."

I let them finish laughing at me, then I said, "Valor. That's what I wanted to talk to you about. Last night, before I fell asleep, I was thinking about what Admiral Nimitz said of the Marines who fought to capture Iwo Jima. 'Uncommon valor was a common virtue.'

"Anyway, it occurred to me that what we got going in our country right now, in politics, in general morality, is that common sense is an absent virtue."

Norb rubbed his chin. "Common sense. It sure ain't common. Notso's right. It don't even exist anymore."

"Yeah," Del said. "Nowadays, there ain't no middle ground. There's the far right and the far left and nothing in between but no-man's land. If you try to go there, to the middle, to try to find a way to compromise, both sides open up on you with everything they got."

"Politics," Oscar said. "It's dirtier than the F-word or even the N-word."

"Of course," I pointed out, "if we were to say politics is dirtier than the N-word, the Political Correctness Police would pillory us."

Oscar grimaced. "I wish you'd speak notso dictionary."

I was about to defend myself when I noticed Oscar smirking. He'd tried to get a rise out of me.

"But, Notso is onto something here," Oscar said. "Politics. In the last two presidential elections, most of us did not vote for either candidate the two parties put forward. One was too hard right, the other too hard left. There was no lesser of evils. So, we didn't vote for either one."

"Then there's PCP," Del said. "Uh, Political Correctness Police, not the drug."

"Just to be safe," Oscar said, "we should give Del a urinalysis."

"Hey," Norb said. "Let's stay on track here. What about the PC Police, Del?"

"Well, you know how if someone says something politically incorrect, the PC Police, just comes down on him, or her, and rips their guts out. In effect, there is no free speech. There's only politically correct speech."

"Here's what happened to me," sez I. "I wasn't sure what I thought about what we talked about yesterday, so I wrote up a summary of our discussion and printed it out. That's when the Squeeze walked in. She wanted to know if I was working on another book and asked if she could read it. Then, without waiting for my assent, or refusal, she pulls the pages out of the printer and returns to the kitchen table.

"Eight minutes later, she's back in the boy-room (She says I'm not grown up enough to have a man-room). She said, 'There are things in here that make me afraid, like the hands-up business and mentioning the N-word.'

"That clinched it for me. If we think something is the truth, and we are afraid to say it, what does it say about us and our country? The Squeeze being afraid to say a politically incorrect truth pushed me over the edge.

"I am for Dispatches from COP Corner, and I propose Dispatch #1 be titled Truth is in the eye of the beholder."

This establishes COP corner. Founding members are: Hiram Mudd, Gregory Normal, Norb Peabody, Del Sanford, Oscar Wexel, and Ollie Fenstermacher.

First, COP does not mean law enforcement officer. No, it stands for Curmudgeonly Old Poop, and this Facebook page represents the National Confederation of COPs, Curmudgeonly Old Poops.

Membership requirements are simple. You have to believe three things:

1. The world is going to hell in a handbasket.
2. The world is hell-bent-for-election to get there.
3. There's not one stinking thing anybody can do about it.

But there's a kicker. Those of us who founded COPs decided there is something we could do about it. It has to do with understanding TRUTH. Truth today is not an absolute. It is in the eye of the beholder.

In our country, we have two polar-opposite truths co-existing, simultaneously, but certainly not peacefully.

What we have is far-left truth; and we have far-right truth; and these two truths stand on opposite sides of the street, shout at each other, and wave signs. If you try to walk down the middle of the street, both sides will close in and beat the snot out of you. As soon as you are silenced, the two sides resume their places, their rants, and shouting their truth.

Us COPs decided we needed our truth to be out there, too. Here's the first thing about truth. There is no absolute truth. That's because there's a truth uncertainty principle, just like the one for quantum physics. That one's called the Heisenberg principle. One of its tenets is that when you are trying to measure something, the act of measuring disturbs the thing you are trying to measure. For example, if you are measuring speed and your speed measuring method tells you the car's speed is 92 MPH, the actual speed is not 92.000000 MPH. It is actually 92 plus or minus some fraction of a MPH, or even whole MPHs.

The corollary for truth goes like this. Measuring absolute truth requires a totally objective mind, one freed of all emotion. Sort of like Joe Friday saying, "Just the facts, Ma'am." Do the far left and far right discourse dispassionately about their truths? Course not. Their truths must be shouted. Signs must be waved. Accepting any fraction of the other side's truth cannot be tolerated. Dispassionate discourse is diabolical surrender to the mortal enemy.

For productive discourse to occur, there must be room for each side to acknowledge that the other side isn't right about all things, but it may be right about some things. And the same thing is true of me. Maybe I'm not right about everything, but I am right about some things.

So, if we can throttle back the passion, maybe we can find some truth in what you are saying, and you might find some in what I'm saying. And what does that sound like?

Why common sense.

Remember what Admiral Nimitz said about the US Marines who captured Iwo Jima? "Uncommon valor was a common virtue."

As to common sense in our country, common sense isn't common, or even an uncommon virtue. It's a non-existent virtue.

A handful of us Poops established COPs Corner last week over lunch at an American Legion Post. When we discussed this topic, common sense, the notion of balance came up. We decided that the way forward for our country rests on a couple of things:

1. Stop shouting and listen.
2. Look for THE truth, not YOUR truth.
3. Work for balance in your outlook.

Funny how things happen. We ended the last dispatch talking about balance. Well, the day after we published Dispatch #1 on our Facebook page, Hiram, one of the Founding Poops, went out to pick up the morning paper.

His delivery person had plopped the rolled St Louis Post Dispatch—they do dispatches, too—about two feet from the edge of the driveway. So, Hiram's bent over and stretched for the paper, trying not to step on the dew-wet grass and mess up his house slippers, when he tumbled, hip-pockets over teakettle. He wound up on his back, staring up at dim Man-In-The Morning-Moon who was laughing his butt off—as if he had one. But then Hiram realizes it wasn't the MITMM laughing. It was his neighbor, Zeke Aaron.

Hiram, on his back, with his slippers still dry, but from nape to buttocks, he was sopping up dew. He was confused for a moment. A whole bunch of thoughts seemed to be just outside his mind. He could see them, but they weren't real thoughts cause he hadn't let them in and thunk 'em yet. One was, Thank You, God, I'm not hurt; and Please, God, don't let Zeke see me; and right behind that was; Oh, crap! He saw. Please, God, fire and brimstone him before he posts a picture of me on Facebook.

Now what happened was Zeke Aaron walked out to get his paper at the same time his across the street neighbor Hiram did. Zeke stepping onto his front porch triggered his motion sensor and turned on his doorbell camera, which caught the whole Hiram walk-over.

Zeke didn't even pick up his paper. He just hurried inside, got the doorbell footage, and posted it before Hiram managed to—gracefully—struggle to his feet—in his then sopping wet slippers.

When he got inside the house, Hiram woke his wife Glenda getting dry underwear out of the dresser and taking them into the bathroom. She got up to see what was going on and caught him pulling on dry skivvies with his wet clothes all in sopping heap in the bathtub.

She shook her head. "Criminy sakes, Hiram. What do I have to do? Find you full body Depends?"

That's when the phone rang. At 5:30 a.m. In the morning!

Hiram's phone rang steady all blinking morning. As the day wore on, more and more people saw Zeke's post and recognized the tumbler and called him forthwith. (I like that word. They use it a lot on

Blue Bloods. I don't get that many opportunities to use it my own self.)

At 8:30 a.m., a Post Dispatch reporter called. That's when Hiram used his cell phone to call an emergency lunch meeting of COPs founders at the Legion Post.

Now when I told the Squeeze about the emergency, she said, "You come home stinking of beer, and we're going to have our own emergency!"

To which I replied, "Yes, Dear."

Anyway, at the Legion, they got their beers, and I got my fizzy water, and we jumped right into discussing our tragedy.

"We're the laughingstock of the whole St. Louis area," Oscar said.

"Yeah, that guy Zeke Aaron posted Hiram's fall from grace on his Facebook page with a link to ours." Del piped in, "This time tomorrow, we'll be the laughingstock of Missouri, Illinois, Kansas, Arkansas, and Iowa. Shoot. Even Ozarks folks'll be laughing at us."

From Norb: "This time tomorrow my hairy heinie! Right now, we're the laughingstock of the world wide web."

Ollie: "This is just terrible. We should pull the plug on COPs Corner. It'll blow over in a couple days."

"It won't blow over. This will be mentioned in each of our obituaries," said Oscar.

"I hope it is," I said.

Hiram hadn't uttered a peep to that point. He'd

been hunkered over his beer, sulking, probably wishing one of us had been humiliated and undermined this great idea we all had. He looked up at me as if he had a knuckle-sandwich he'd made just for me.

"This is exactly the kind of thing we talked about in our first dispatch," Me again. "We talked about balance, but not physical balance. In COPs, the O stands for old. Lots of us have physical balance issues. It's why our wives won't let us climb ladders anymore. Half of us use canes and the other half ought to.

"But! But we got more than a thousand responses to Dispatch #1. One said, 'We should listen to these COPs tell us about balance?' Then he showed the clip of Hiram take his tumble a hundred times in a row.

"We were talking about an entirely different kind of balance. The kind we were talking about is mental. moral … and spiritual. But see what happened? The other side just jumped on the word balance, and even though our meaning was obvious, they manufactured their own truth about our dispatch.

"Hiram, nothing on God's green earth could serve Dispatches from COP Corner any better. After Dispatch #2, I bet we get ten thousand responses. I do feel bad for you, that you are bearing the brunt of the repercussions, but this is what I'm proposing."

I started outlining what I thought should be in Dispatch #2, when Norb said he needed another beer. The others did, too. The bartender brought us more beer. And one stupid fizzy water. Everybody at the table liked the plan, and we set to refining it, which called for another round, which was a mistake.

In all the excitement over figuring a way out of the pit of humiliation, we'd forgotten what our original name was: Wednesday-lunch-at-the-America-Legion-<u>two-beers-only</u> guys.

See, all of us wear support socks. Half of us wear knee highs, but me and the other half wear pantyhose supports over our Depends. Now, the men's restroom in the Legion consists of a long trough and one stall. When I was on my fourth fizzy, and the others were finishing fourth beers, we all got up and headed for the loo at the same time. Of course, the trough-ers got right down business. Which added to us panty-hosers discomfit. But, after what had happened to Hiram, Oscar and me decided he could use the stall first. When he entered and closed the door, Oscar and I crossed our legs and hoped he'd hurry, but then he said "Ahhh."

Me and Oscar suffered sympathetic relaxations.

We concluded the meeting right there in the latrine with a decision that I would write up two potential second dispatches. If the Post Dispatch published an article about Hiram's acrobatics, one version would address the article. If the Post D. didn't run such an article, the other version would address that case.

Plus, we sure hoped like all get-out Zeke Aaron hadn't hidden a camera in the WC, or head, or what the heck, bathroom.

Ex-military men didn't say bathroom. Unless, of course, you had a grandson with you who needed to go.

Anyway, I walked to my car like a two-year-old with a diaper-full and drove home. And got myself shipshape again. And went to work on the two Dispatches #2.

There was something Freudianly bothersome about that #2.

The Founding Poops are delighted with the response to our first dispatch. DEEEE LIGHTED. Here's what happened?

We wrote about truth, common sense, and balanced outlooks. The next day, one of us fell hip-pockets over teakettle picking up his newspaper. His neighbor's doorbell camera caught the botched walk-over attempt. Friendly neighbor then posted the video poking fun at the well-balanced-flat-on-his-backside Old Poop. And everyone out there in web-land jumped onboard and heaped more ridicule on him. And, by association, the rest of us COPs as well. One comment said we were more mentally crippled than physically.

Mind you, not one of us Founders consider ourselves to be a cripple. Half of us, though, qualify to park in those special spots, but we'd rather park so far away from the grocery store entrance we'd have to take Uber to get there than to park in a I ain't-as-spry-as-I-used-to-be spot.

On the other hand, I personally have seen a

number of perfectly healthy young people, of both sexes, some wearing workout clothing, and spry as all get-out, use those reserved parking spots. However, I have not seen very many males use spots reserved for expectant mothers. So, some of us have boundaries. At any rate, it made me wonder how many of the people who on-line laughed at fell-flat-on-his-backside-old man have ever used a only-for-those-with-a-disability space. And I wonder where they got the okay-to-park-in-such-a-spot-rearview-mirror dangly. Did they print it for themselves? Did they steal it from a wheelchair bound grandmother?

Back to the matter at hand: balance. In Dispatch #1, we were obviously writing about mental, moral, emotional, objective balance. But that doorbell cam video provided the perfect opportunity to laugh at the subject at hand, rather than deal with it. Dealing with it might involve work. It could mean I'd have to change.

Change. Another subject. See how this kind of discussion presents so many opportunities to sidetrack off the topic at hand, in this case balance. But the shouters in our country, one side anyway, clamors for CHANGE. Implying that the world isn't going to hell in a handbasket. No. It is already there. The old must be thrown out and something brand new created. Never mind there is no ready solution being shouted. Other than to defund the police. Defund the police at a time when the mentality and morality of the crowd rampages in our streets with anarchy around the next corner? That's YOUR solution? YOUR truth?

On the other side of the change issue, there are those who shout, "If it ain't broke, don't fix it." "Leave things the way they are." "It doesn't matter if there are mass shootings every week, you ain't touching my freedom to bear arms." Here's the thing. There are extraordinarily powerful weapons available to every Tom, Dick, and Gloria in our country today, that it can't be too long before most of the country is adding onto their garages to hold their tank.

More about this in a subsequent Dispatch.

Here's a thing about our American form of government. The Founding Fathers strove to find, not a perfect form of governing, rather, a more perfect form of governing, a more perfect union to provide for the common good. A better common good than would be possible without it. They acknowledged, that in the past, previous forms of government turned into funnels channeling power into the hands of an elite class of opportunistic exploiters. The Founding Fathers created a system with checks and balances, to try and prevent one segment of government from grabbing an unbalanced share of power.

Founding Fathers begs the question: Would our present form of government be better if there had been Founding Fathers AND Mothers? Perhaps. But in the opinion of the COPs, the Fathers laid out a good set of BALANCED principles. From those principles, they set out to form a more perfect union.

Not a perfect one. But one that strives to get as close to perfection as possible for humans with limited capacity for objectivity. History teaches us that for most human endeavors, there will be at least two widely differing opinions as to how to get the job done.

Someone will say, "We agree that we need to get this done, right?"

Voices murmur assent.

Someone #1 says, "Well, then. How about if we do it this way?"

After a seven-second pause, Someone #2 says, "Hold on. How about if we do it that way?"

In the ensuing dialogue volleying this way and that way back and forth, the minds of the decision makers settle on one way or the other. Further discussion slices away the extremes of the initial two ideas until a middle notion is settled on. A vote settles the matter. A modified that way wins.

A this-way supporter mumbles, "Boogers."

A that-way supporter claps him on the back and says, "Never mind, Obadiah, you'll win the next one. And you have to admit, what we decided makes the nation better. Not totally better, maybe, but some better. Right?"

"Well, yeah," Obadiah grumbles.

Make the nation better. Through discussion, weighing merits of this and that way, and voting. A more perfect union.

Now consider today.

Far Left and Far Right shout at each other. Both sides minds are closed to compromise.

We as a nation need to do something about that.

We, the people, need to change our my-way-or-the-highway views more than our form of government needs to change.

One last thought. Founding Mothers. You can search the web and find that writers have compiled a list of them. If the list wouldn't be out there already, we COPS would have started our own list with Martha Washington being number one.

Picture George Washington. He's getting dressed for his inauguration address, and he comes downstairs. Martha takes one look at him. "For pity sakes, George. You forgot to put in your wooden teeth."

George's valet was worried about getting his wig on straight, and his butler worried about brushing the wig powder from his shoulders. The valet worried if he had his vest buttoned. The butler worried if he had it buttoned properly. The valet worried about the polish on his boots. The butler worried about spots on his white pants.

What would have happened if Martha hadn't noticed the missing teeth?

Picture this. George walks up to the podium and those closest to the stage notice the missing chompers and begin giggling and telling those behind them. The father of our country is laughed off the stage. Our more perfect union comes apart at the seams. Like a sailing ship sliding down the launching rails, into the water, breaking in half, and sinking with the mast poking above the water, a monument to what could have been.

We COPs believe that behind every great man, there is a woman rolling her eyes, and making sure the man is dressed properly before he presents himself in public. We COPs remember and honor Martha as the Mother of our country just as we remember and honor the Father.

Ain't that a kick in the mouth? Doesn't that thought just reek of balance?

A last last thought. Our objective in this dispatch, even if a thousand people laugh at it, is get one person to read it with listening eyes.

HISTORY OF COP CORNER, #3

Of all the things which might have elicited responses, the one which generated the most comments was our use of the word cripple. Just some of the responses: "Demeaning;" "Insulting;" "Belittling;" "Total lack of concern for people with disabilities;" "What you'd expect from a bunch of Neanderthal troglodytes;" and "Curmudgeonly Old Poops should neither be seen nor heard."

At our next COP meeting, Hiram jumped in with, "One of them said, 'You COPs are more crippled mentally than physically.' But did that comment generate even one peep of protest from the pack of Politically Correct hyenas out there? It did not!"

That input from Hiram woke us some.

"Those, those, those—" Norb sputtered, like his lawnmower just putted to life and then quit because the gas tank was empty.

"They judged what we said based on who said it," Oscar said. "Not what we said."

"They've already judged what we ain't even wrote yet," Ollie fumed.

Now it had been my intention to suggest to The-Curmudgeonly-Old-Poops-Wednesday-two-beers-only-lunch bunch that we take on discussion of the word cripple in our next dispatch. But I sure didn't need to prime that pump.

"No matter what we put in a future Dispatch, it's sure as shootin' gonna' git web-shouted down," Del stormed.

Our communal outrage meter was already pegged at the high-end of the scale. Our united we-won't-stand-for-this flat broke the outrage-meter needle.

Our adrenalin-juiced rants included: "Who the Sam Hill do these young whippersnappers—" "Over-privileged, over-entitled, never had to work for a single thing in their whole lives." "Yeah, they had everything handed to them on a silver platter, and they believe the world owes them to continue to do that in perpetuity."

After that last one, Oscar grimaced, like he does now and then. "I wish you'd speak notso dictionary."

Anyway, this was looking like it was going to be a long discussion. I remembered what happened last time when we forgot to count our beers and fizzy waters, so as the others ordered second beers, I went to the WC. Trying to keep ahead of the insistent call-of-nature beast. But to no avail. I sat there with my panty-hose support stockings around my ankles and produced nothing. I guess there's a law of Physics that says it is not possible to control your bladder, rather, your bladder controls you.

By the time I got myself together again and

returned to the table, the discussion had ratcheted up to hyper-warble. The table was, to a man, mightily torqued off.

Norb was saying, "Those … those … those young entitled don't-have-a-mind-of-their-own … whippersnappers."

"We need a name for them," Ollie said.

"Young, entitled, don't-have-a-mind-of-their-own," Norb said, and then he tacked on the last word which just squirted loathing into our ears, "whippersnappers."

I took my seat and found myself caught up in this project. "We need something shorter. The attention span of these whippersnappers is no more than three words long."

"Well," Del said, as he poised his ballpoint above a pad of paper, "let's list the key characteristics of these whippersnappers. Then we can pick the three best words."

I jumped right in with, "Entitled." Del wrote it.

"Young," from our scribe.

"Mindless," Ollie offered. "You know, they don't think. They get their ideas from the web. Somebody posts something out there like 'I'm outraged, and you need to be, too!' Nobody stops to ask, "Is that really true?' No. They just jump on board with the idea and start chasing down whoever has been declared guilty ready to lynch the guy."

"Classic," I said. "The Oxbow Incident."

"What's that?" from Hiram.

"It's a book," I reply, ready to explain the story.

"And a movie," Norb cuts in.

"Starring Henry Fonda," says Ollie. "And William Eythe."

"Sounded like you got a lisp and were trying to say ice," Del said.

Ollie choked on his beer, and Norb pounded him on the back.

"The guy's name is William Ithe." Ollie was indignant. "E-Y-T-H-E. How would you pronounce it?"

"I wouldn'ta pronounced it at all. William Eythe? Who the hell is he? Henry Fonda. Just leave it with him."

"I've got Oxbow on VHS," Ollie said. "I watch it a lot. I see that guy's name in the credits. Never seen a name like that before. I just think it's a cool name."

"Guys!" I said. "Stop. Do you know what we were doing just before William E-Y-T-H-E cut in?" All eyes were on me. "I know what we should post in Dispatch #3."

Through the rest of the discussion, we orchestrated trips to the head. This was way bigger than a two-beers-only palaver. We also agreed that we'd all rent the movie and watch it that night, so tomorrow, when I had the dispatch ready to review, we'd all have the lesson from the movie firmly fixed in our minds.

Discussing D #3 took us beyond Jeopardy. When I got home, the first thing I got was a sniff test from the Squeeze. I hadn't had one beer, much less two.

Just stupid fizzy water, but that pleased the Squeeze. She, on the spot, upgraded my boy-room to a teen-aged-male-of-the-species room.

We had a nice dinner, the Squeeze and me. Then I retired to my more-mature-than-it-used-to-be room and did some writin'.

The response to our Dispatch #2 was a widespread condemnation of our use of the word cripple. An interesting thing happened to us COPS as we discussed the reactions to Dispatch #2. All of us Founding COPs got caught up in a communal outrage because, in a response to Dispatch #1, one of the respondents said, "You COPs are more mentally crippled than physically." But did that spark even a single criticism over use of that apparently Politically Incorrect word. (Note: caps intended.) It DID NOT.

We were torqued off. It was so unfair. And we were not going to stand for it. As our outrage mounted, we all agreed on one thing. We did not have a name for our enemies, our respondents. And we felt the need, the need for a name that held more poop in it than our own name. We were tossing around name ideas, and things like over-privileged whippersnappers, over entitled whippersnappers. Go-along-with-the-crowd whippersnappers.

Ollie called up the definition of whippersnapper on his phone and read it to us: "An unimportant but offensively presumptuous person, especially a young one."

Norb said, "Perfect. We don't need to tack on any of the other stuff. Whippersnapper perfectly describes those … those—"

"Whippersnappers," Del suggested.

To a man we exulted in having nailed those unimportant but offensively presumptuous young persons.

"What's wrong with them," one of us said, "is that none of them think for themselves. Somebody posts an idea on the web, and they all jump on board with the idea, even though it's outrageous and nobody stops to ask, "Is this true? Has this been fact checked?"

"Right," another of us said. "The Whippersnappers are The-Oxbow-Incident lynch mob personified. Hang the suspected rustlers, then fact check."

At this point, one of us said, "Guys. Guys. See what we're doing? We're doing just what we were upset about them doing. They stuck a bumper sticker on our butts that said, "Neanderthal troglodyte." Remember that one response to Dispatch #1? Well, we just tattooed "Whippersnapper" on their snow-white cheeks."

At our table of Curmudgeonly Old Poops, in the Legion Hall, we had a pregnant pause.

After a bit, one of us said, "Don't that beat all? Sure is easy to get all caught up in something like this. Even calm, objective, rational thinkers such as ourselves got all fired up to lynch us some whippersnappers."

One of us laughed. Then we all did. Laughed at ourselves. Once the laughter died down, we had, in our own opinion, some objective discussion.

The first thing we talked about was flinging about the term whippersnapper. The way we used it, it was meant to be wounding, to put those offensively presumptuous children in their place.

Del told us about the homily his preacher delivered the previous Sunday. One of the items he covered was driving. "How many of us," the homilist proposed, "have had a driver in front of us sit at a traffic light that just went green, and even horns honking doesn't get him to move before he finishes his text? And when that happens, what do we do? The preacher said, "I'll tell you what I do, if no one is in the car with me, I cuss him to high heaven out loud. If someone is in car with me, I cuss him to high heaven in my thoughts." The preacher went on to suggest, that in situations like that, instead of giving in to the impulse to cuss another human being out, forgive him. Right then and there on the spot. And even though by the time you get to move, you missed the green light entirely. Forgive Mr. Text-man. And pray that the next time, he might find it in his soul to have a bit of concern for his fellow man, or woman, driver, that he might not do unto others what he would not want others to do unto him.

The preacher wrapped up with, "Do you see what would happen if we could forgive instead of curse? Why we'd be pumping love and compassion into the atmosphere over our planet, not more hate. And make no mistake. It is not some shade of gray torqued-off feeling we are talking about, it is black as sin hate that such behavior at a traffic light stands on."

We spent a lot of time talking about what that preacher said. Then we made some decisions.

One of our decisions, apologize for even thinking, and then calling some of you out there in web-land whippersnappers. We the COPs, hereby, officially apologize.

And we apologize for two things.

First, we apologize for calling you an insulting, demeaning name.

Second, we apologize for allowing ourselves to be caught up in the very thing we were sermonizing against. That is slip into crowd-mind. Become part of a crowd and let the crowd decide the right and wrong of things. And not in a shade of gray sense. No, in terms of blatant black versus pure as the driven snow white. Unequivocal right, and unequivocal wrong.

The thing that is wrong with crowd-mind is that it takes in a thimbleful of evidence, huffs up with indignation, then decides: We have to do something about this! And rushes off and grabs the first people they come upon who look to the crowd-mind like they might be rustlers. And they hang them forthwith.

That's just what we did when we hung the whippersnapper moniker on some of You People. And we ask You People to forgive Us People.

We talked about this at the Legion. We decided

there is currently a divide between us, and we need some way to talk about ourselves on both sides of the divide. So we came up with You People and Us People as a way to label the parties involved. We further resolved that what we are after with our Dispatches, is that You People and Us People become We The People. To bridge the gap between us, we have to bridle the passions of the wild stallions we are riding who would stampede us in one direction or another. And that will take some work. It is so easy to let those wild stallions go where they will, but to rein in the passions of the beast, we have to work to guide the animal where we would have it take us.

Us People pledge to You People that we will endeavor to do just that, to rein in our passions, to discuss with open minds the issues that divide us.

We started out talking about use of the term cripple, but this dispatch has gotten long enough, and we will pick up that discussion in next the Dispatch.

We also refined the membership requirements for COPs.

COPs must believe:

The world is going to hell in a handbasket.

It is hell-bent-for-election to get there.

There IS something we can do about.

Find one opportunity to forgive an annoying dweeb every day.

COPs must watch The Oxbow Incident movie or read the book. Doing both is best.

HISTORY OF COP CORNER, #4

A funny thing happened to me, Gregory George Notso Normal, COP Corner historian and Dispatch drafter. The day we issued Dispatch #3, My One and Only Squeeze told me at dinner that she read it. And liked it. And here's the funny, well, the amazing thing, really. The Squeeze looked at me with admiration gushing out of her soft brown eyes.

Now the Squeeze and me love the crap out of each other. We have since the end of junior year in high school, sixty-four years ago. But I was pretty sure I never saw admiration in her eyes before. I was gobsmacked. That look of hers inseminated feelings in me I hadn't experienced in a decade. I excused myself to go to the bathroom. Did I have any of those little blue pills left?

I had some left! Joy, joy, joy!

But wait. The use by date was eight and a half years ago. Rat snot!

What's the worst thing that could happen? I could die. Well, yeah, but I'd die happy.

✦✦✦✦✦

The next day being Friday, we officially changed our name from The Wednesday-lunch-at-the-American-Legion-two-beers-only guys to Tuesday-through-Friday-lunch-at-the-American-Legion-two-beers-most-of-the-time guys. Dealing with the Dispatches and the reactions was not a one-day-a-week job.

I arrived first. Then Hiram and Oscar came in and both were ebullient. Babbling and gabbling like high school freshman girls who just came from gym class conducted by the new, hot-hunk new men's basketball coach. Now Hiram's a six-footer and has a beefy torso propped on sturdy legs. Oscar looks a lot like him, except he's only five-six. Like God was going to build them to be twins only He ran out of parts before He finished the job with Twin Two. Oscar said something and Hiram rubbed a big paw over Oscar's shiny-bald-on-top head. Which usually made Oscar mad. Not that day, though. He was so ebullient he couldn't get mad.

I was kind of ebullient my own self, and I was pretty sure I knew what happened to them.

As Mutt and Jeff took their seats, Norb and Ollie came in. They were ebullient, too. Both of them are about five-ten, but exact opposites with the rest of their features. Norb's skinny. Ollie's fat. Norb wears a crew cut. Ollie wears his hair long and sports a man bun, but they were twins in the ebullience department.

Norb scooted around the side of his chair and sat. Now what he used to do ten years ago was to hike his leg over the chairback like he was mounting a horse.

Being eighty ain't a little bit older than seventy. It's a lotta' bit older. Anyway, he says, "Your wives tell you what they did yesterday?"

The Squeeze didn't say anything about what she did. The only thing I remembered of yesterday was she smiled at me with admiration. And holy crap invitation! And after, I lay there on my pillow grinning up to heaven like a kid who just got a pony for his birthday. She sighed, turned on her side, and went to sleep. I grinned for quite a while longer. And it had been quite a while. Since the early part of the last decade. I'd come to believe that that time seven, eight, nine years ago had been the last time ever. But the bothersome thing was, I couldn't remember exactly when it had happened or any other detail about it. But, tonight, I'd remember, and treasure it, and smile ebulliently with each remembering.

"Earth to Notso. Earth to Notso. You hear what Norb said?" from Ollie.

"Uh. Well. The Squeeze didn't say nuthin' about what she … they did."

Norb grinned. "Rhonda told me, during pillow talk, you know? Anyway, she said they all went to lunch at the St. Louis Bread Company. They have these salads with fruit in it during the summer, and they all love it."

"Even if it's called fruit salad, fruit is for dessert," said Hiram.

"As I was sayin', before being interrupted, our wives went to lunch together. They talked about us, about what we put in the last dispatch. About forgiving the dweeb at the traffic light who holds everybody up because he doesn't see the light's gone green cause he's busy texting. Rhonda said they all figured that was the most mature thing any of us had done in our whole married life."

Which for us COPs ranged from thirty-seven to fifty-nine years.

Norb shook his head. "They all figured our brains went into permanent arrested development at puberty, and there was no hope our little one-track minds would ever display such rational, compassionate thinking. To a woman, they were surprised, but even more, proud of us.

"Ollie's Molly proposed that they form a COPs Ladies Auxiliary."

"Do we get a say?" Oscar said. "Do Curmudgeonly Old Poops want a Ladies Auxiliary?"

"Rhonda said it's a done deal. They agreed to a charter for the Auxiliary right there in the Bread Company. They're going to setup a Facebook page and a website and start a blog."

Little Oscar huffed himself up to close to Hiram size. "Now just you wait a fribble-frappin', stink-bombin', snot-waddin' minute! We just got Dispatches runnin'. Are we gonna let them wimmen shanghai our idea and turn it inside out? We can't let that happen!"

I felt Ebullience get ready to vacate the premises. Before it did, I grabbed off my personal hunk of it and stuck it in a trunk in the attic of my brain. Losing the whole rest of my mind wouldn't matter. Long as I held onto that memory.

The conversation heated up some, and we even forgot to order lunch, but Ted Tapman, the bartender, kept us supplied with beer and stupid fizzy water. And when the non-COP lunch-bunch started leaving the post, Bill Baker the cook brought us bowls of Son-of-a-gun stew. So, for a while the conversation got a little harder to understand because we were all talking with our mouths full. And spitting bits of food at each other. Not on purpose, mind you, but we were het up some that the wimmen wanted to take over COP Corner.

By the time we'd mopped our plates clean with bread and et that, we all had little gobs of food stuck to our shirts. But we'd decided what to do. We were going to have a Saturday lunch meeting with the women in the Legion Post meeting room, so's we'd have us some privacy when we laid down the law to our better halves.

That's when Del walked in. At 3 p.m. He had a serious look on his face. Now Del, most times, sports a serious look. But this was a serious, serious look. He's about five-ten, and it's easy to think of him as skinny. But he was a SEAL, and his arms and shoulders pack more strength and power than many a majorly pumped-up muscleman.

"Something wrong?"

Del nodded.

Rat snot! I was hoping I'd make it home for

Jeopardy for a change. But Del's mouth motor is like a motorcycle engine that likes to try to wear out the kick starter. Takes some time to get his mouth motor humming. But I sure wanted to know what'd upset him. I could see the others wanted to know, too.

Del was on his second beer when he started talking. Before coming to the Legion Post for lunch, his Eunice had him drive to church to drop off a quilt the Ladies Sodality made to raffle off at the upcoming parish picnic. Well, Del stops at the stoplight at First Capital and Fifth Streets behind this Chevy pickup on honking big wheels.

Del's story took a while, so, yeah, I missed Jeopardy. Again!

But after Del finished his story, I told the guys I knew what needed to go in the next Dispatch. They ruminated on it for a good minute.

"Yeah," Little Oscar said.

Big Hiram nodded. So did Skinny Norb. Ollie's fat head dipped a bit and twitched sideways a bit. Sort of like exactly half ways between a nod of assent and a head shake meaning "Not only no, but hell no." As if he didn't know what we were voting on, but he didn't want to be left out of the voting.

"The ayes have it," I said.

"We still meeting with the wimmen tomorra?" Ollie said.

Hiram grimaced. "Maybe we should hold off on that."

Fat Ollie said, "Yeah. We should hold off on that."

"Y'all're afraid to lay the law down to your significant other?" Skinny Norb posited.

Sawed-off Oscar said, "If you ain't got no valor, you best have a boatload of discretion."

We did not meet with the wimmen the next day.

Isn't that the way of things? You stumble across a universal truth and figure it should decide for you your action and response to a particular circumstance every time this circumstance arises.

Be sitting at a red traffic light behind another car. It turns green, but the first vehicle does not move. Instead of honking at the dweeb, you forgive him. Say a prayer for him.

Exactly that circumstance happened to one of our founding COPs yesterday. A pickup truck with honking big wheels had stopped for a red. Founding Member pulls up behind him. The light goes green, but does Honking-big Wheels move on through the intersection? It does not. It sits there. Founding Member wrestles his indignation into submission, and he asks the Lord to bless the driver of the truck, and to help him find a way to consider his fellow drivers when he next gets behind the wheel. That's when the car behind Founding Member honked its horn.

In his rearview mirror, Founding Member saw a thirty-something soccer mom in a minivan with a boatload of kids. Then she just leaned on the horn. Made a heck of a racket. The driver door of the pickup flew open, and this guy who looked like Hulk Hogan jumped out. To Founding Member, Hulk carried what looked like a Dirty Harry handgun. You know, the most powerful handgun in the universe, and it can blow your head clean off. Soccer Mom stopped honking. Hulk started stomping toward Founding Member's car with his shoulders hunched up. The man wore a black leather wife-beater and ugly face hair.

Founding Member undid his seatbelt, unlocked his door, and rolled his window down.

Hulk stopped and pointed his pistol at Founding Member. "Pisses me off to get honked at. This is a .44 Magnum, the most powerful handgun in the universe. It can blow your head clean off. I've a mind to do just that."

Founding Member noted the .44 had been cocked and the man had his finger inside the finger guard. Also, the man's pupils were dilated. Drugs, FM thought.

"It wasn't me," Founding Member said. "It was the car behind me."

Hulk glared.

Now FM, as I mentioned earlier, wears a serious look on his face. The other thing his face wears is a sincere look. Like he couldn't lie if his life depended on it.

So Ugly Face Hair snaps his glare back at Soccer

Mom. He glances back at Mr. Sincerity; then he takes one step toward the minivan.

Now the lane next to FM was a left-turn lane. A car was approaching in that lane. FM opened his door and slammed it into Hulk hurling him in front of left-turn car. There's a screech of brakes and a thump. Hulk winds up on his back next to the hanging-open door of his pickup.

Del stepped out onto the street and picked up the .44. He let the hammer down, unloaded the pistol, then tossed it into his car as he pocketed the bullets. Walking over to Hulk, he saw the man had a compound fracture of his left arm. The man's black eyes had lost that depraved-indifference-to-the-value-of-human-life look and were now chock full of fear. His breaths came in short huffs. Busted rib punctured his lung maybe. That's what FM thought. He also thought the guy was a threat to no one just then. So, he called 911.

When Anonymous Founding Member joined us non-anonymous members and told us what happened, we amended our COP membership requirements. Since these requirements are principles members must embrace, we decided to call these principles COP Creed.

COP Creed:

1. The world is going to hell in a handbasket.
2. It is hell-bent-for-election to get there.

3. There IS something we can do about.
4. Find one opportunity to forgive an annoying dweeb every day.
5. COPs must watch The Oxbow Incident movie or read the book. Doing both is best.
6. Number four above does not apply if the dweeb is packing a gun.

At our next Tuesday meeting, we founding COPs scratched our heads for a bit trying to figure out what issue to deal with next. Between the first and second beer, and stupid fizzy water, Hiram told a story about something that happened to him at the grocery store the day before. In the checkout line. A woman had perceived him as being crippled.

I stopped listening to Hiram, because his story brought to mind something that had happened to me a few weeks back. My One and Only Squeeze and I have season tickets to the MUNY, an outdoor theater in St. Louis. They have metal detectors you have to pass through. The guy in front of me had a cane, which set off the alarm. I didn't have a cane and passed through without setting off a peep. But when I cleared the metal detector, one of the MUNY attendants asked if I needed a wheelchair to get to my seat.

"No," I said, and I think I said it nice. Though I was miffed that young woman thought I was so crippled I needed a wheelchair. Being thought I was crippled rankled through the whole show. It was Sweeney Todd. By the end of the show, I was ready to hire the barber of Fleet Street to go after that young woman by the metal detector. He'd teach her to not think people were crippled when they weren't.

But here's the thing. I had been working like heck so people would not see me as crippled. And in my mind, what I had been doing worked. For six years. Then I turned eighty, and at least to that MUNY attendant, what I'd been doing didn't work anymore.

For another beer's worth, Hiram and I talked about how hard we worked at not being perceived as crippled. Then Oscar and Norb, the two guys who use canes, gave us an insight we weren't expecting.

Del said, "We wrote about the term 'crippled' in Dispatch Number One, but I don't think we adequately closed that subject out."

"What about it, Notso?" Ollie said. "You got stuff to write about in a draft for the next Dispatch?"

"Yeah. Yeah, I do."

"Good," Ollie said, and ordered another round of beers. And one stupid fizzy water.

We, the founding COPs, decided we hadn't dealt adequately with the word "cripple" in our first Dispatch. So here we go. We're going to begin by relating stories of two of our members who've had experience dealing with crippled-ness. Or maybe not dealing with it.

Number one tale: Hiram Mudd was grocery shopping last Monday. He entered the checkout-counter line behind this sixty-something, trim, gray-haired Black lady. The way she was turned out, she was a cut above middle class is what he thought. Anyway, Cut-above turns and notices Hiram behind her. Her eyes sweep him from buzz cut to shoe tops and up again.

"Go on. You go ahead of me."

That blew Hiram's socks off. A woman of grandmotherly age offered him head of the line. And she only had three items in her hands while Hiram pushed a cartful of stuff.

Now Mr. Mudd, as previously reported, is not the most graceful of men. Physically. But here's his response: "Ma'am, I thank you kindly. I guess it's obvious I use my shopping cart as a crutch, and I guess it's also obvious I gimp along on my gimpy left leg even with the cart. But I won't let my brain accept any notion about me being crippled. I don't even want to think about how crippled I look to other people. I've trained my brain to flush such thoughts clean out of my head the instant they appear. So, I don't really think of myself that way. Crippled, you know? And really, I am not as crippled as I look.

"But, here's what I propose. I will take your place in line and thank you kindly." Which he did. Then he said, "Ma'am, you only have three items in your hands, and I've got all this. How about if you go ahead of me. If you do that, it will help me feel like a gentleman, which I'm not. Not near often enough."

Cut-above resumed her original place in line. She smiled at Hiram as she left the store. Hiram was smiling, too, when he walked out.

Tale Two is about me, Gregory George Notso Normal. My first experience with being crippled happened six years ago. I was downstairs in our family room with our oldest daughter watching a TV show. She's a nurse. When the show ended, we walked toward the stairs with me leading the way. From behind me I hear, "Holy crap, Dad! You're wonky."

Wonky! What the heck did that mean?

Nurse daughter pointed to my reflection in a window. As I walked, I was way tilted toward my right side, like a Leaning Tower of Pisa with stumpy little legs. Holy crap all right! I had no idea I was wonky. Which was a step beyond crippled in my mind. Sort of like Donald Trump, I thought. Or maybe a mirror image of him. I did not want to be crippled, so I wasn't. I picture The Donald as having been born with a fully developed case of industrial-strength hubris. But the kind of hubris that was visited on mere mortals wasn't enough for his inflated sense of self-worth, so for himself, he developed hubris plus.

> Note: Two of the founding members
> did not want to use the Trump example
> of self-delusion, but four did.

Back to six years ago, I did not want people to see me as wonky. After my daughter left, I went in the bathroom and looked at myself in the mirror. I was wonky all right. Leaned over to the right a considerable amount. Now I'd discovered I had one leg shorter than the other thirty-four years prior. Back then, though, I didn't look wonky. I was straight up and down. I have pictures to prove it. My gig-line had always been straight, too. Perfectly so. Gig-line: the line at the edge of your shirt, next to the buttons, aligned with the edge of your fly. In Officer Candidate School, a screwed-up gig-line earned demerits. Even though I had one leg shorter than the other, I stood straight and tall and my gig-line was picture perfect. But not no longer. Now the stupid gig-line drew an "S" from top to bottom.

Judas priest! What will people think of me? One more way Gregory George is Notso Normal.

I got a couple of books and took them into the bathroom and stood on one, about three-quarters-of-an-inch thick. Didn't even come close to leveling me out. It took two inches worth of books before my shoulders were level in the mirror.

The next day, I took a pair of shoes to a shoe-repair guy and asked him to put a two-inch lift on the right. I had to wait an anxious week to get them back. And, boy, was I happy when the shoes were ready.

I will confess to you my brothers—and sisters—walking with that one lifted shoe felt, well, wonky. But I stuck with it. As long as I didn't look wonky. About a week into wearing my new shoe, the Squeeze said, "George, now you're leaning to the left."

Downstairs to the bathroom. Sure enough. Leaning left, and now the gig line made a backwards "S". Rat snot!

The next day I went to see my doctor for a regular checkup. I told her what I'd done and demonstrated the shoes for her.

"Judas fribble-frapping priest," or words to that effect, she said, and then scheduled me for physical therapy forthwith.

PT and me worked on it for two months. We started with inserts into short-leg-shoe and worked our way up to a three-quarter inch lift. My PT person didn't think we should add more. She was concerned what more lift would do to my spine and my hips and knees. But that three-quarter incher seemed to do the trick. For about five years. Then I turned eighty, and even with the lifted shoe, I got wonky again.

Doc sent me to PT again. I asked PT Person about cranking up the lift. "Another half inch?"

She acted like she didn't even hear what I said. Questions came at me faster than at a perp being sweated by two cops in interrogation. Aches, pains, discomforts, balance? A gazillion questions about those four things and a few others. Like a fool, I answered truthfully. Then she had me walk in front of her. She also had me do some stretches as she watched me like a cat playing with a mouse.

Then she laid it on me. "Add more lift?" She shook her head. "Your body has gotten used to us pushing your posture closer to upright. If we push more, the aches and pains you feel will be ten times worse." Then she really laid it on me. "You need a cane."

Gack! A cane. Cripples need canes. Old cripples! Well, I'm sure as shootin' notso old, and I am not a cripple!

What I was thinking must have shown on my face. PT Person said, "Suit yourself. See the lady at the desk to check out."

That, I decided, was rude and harsh.

Checked out with Lady-at-the-desk check-out Person. Walked out to the pickup, hiked my short leg up, grabbed the steering wheel, hauled my butt onto the seat, hoisted in the long leg, closed the door, stuck the key in the slot, almost turned it to Engine Start, but I stopped.

Call Hiram. A Whisper. Is it my guardian angel or one of the devil's evil spirits who prowl about the world seeking the ruin of souls, amen?

It was a whisper. The devil's minions always shout. Angel then.

I called Hiram. I told him I thought I might be crippled.

Hiram talked. I talked. He talked some more. I did, too. By the time we were done with the back-and-forthing, forty-five minutes had zipped by.

I confessed to my talk-mate that I was a vainglorious, self-delusional, pants-on-fire liar. Our mutual examination of my conscience disclosed two inescapable facts: I was crippled; I was old.

The crippled bit. Ever since #1 kid told me I was wonky, I did everything I could to minimize how wonky, how crippled I looked to other people. Heck, if I'd have had a leg shot off, I probably would have worn a floor-length dress to hide that fact. But the thing is, I was spending enormous moral, emotional, and intellectual energy on convincing myself I wasn't crippled.

And old. Some years back, I trained myself to only look in the mirror for four things: to shave, to comb my hair, to clip nose hairs, and make sure my gig-line was as straight as I could make it. And when I looked in the mirror, I trained my eyes to only look at hair, nose hair, gig line, and shaving cream. Those eyeballs of mine obeyed. That was my secret of eternal youth. Visual evidence of aging, if any were present, my well-trained orbs of observation would not gaze in its direction. And if my eyes inadvertently stumbled across such visual evidence, delete, delete, delete happened to the image before it could be transmitted to the brain.

So, I was young, and eternally so.

"It's right there in our name," Hiram pointed out. "Curmudgeonly OLD Poop. See?"

"Well, yeah, but I thought it meant ole, you know. Like good ole boys."

"Not so, Notso."

Snot-wadding Hiram wasn't going to let me off the hook. He shamed me into not letting myself off the hook.

"It's easy to see faults in others," Hiram said. "It is way easier to hide your own faults from yourself."

Huh! I sure found it easier to see Donald Trump's hubris plus than I saw my own character flaw.

Before hanging up, I told Hiram we needed an emergency meeting of the COPs.

The next day at the Legion Post, Hiram and I told the rest of them about the conversation we had. After that conversation, we both realized we were crippled. Crippled. Not handicapped. Not disabled, but crippled. That's how we thought of ourselves. Not so crippled we'd apply for a crippled rear-view-mirror dangly or a license plate, mind you, but crippled.

Hiram and I both felt we had to see our condition in all its stark reality to be able to deal with it.

And now, Hiram and I both feel like we are dealing with being crippled. Before, we both spent all our effort in not dealing with it. Me, I was sure if I admitted I was crippled I would have esteem issues as ginormous as Eeyore's. But it didn't happen that way. I feel relieved. I no longer have to expend all that energy fooling myself.

Self, I told myself, you're crippled. Deal with it and move on. That simple, see?

At that point in our meeting, Norb piped in with, "If you use a cane, people will pity you less."

What? I'd seen it just the other way.

"He's right," Oscar said. "People can tell if you're crippled whether you use a cane or not. If you use one, they think you are doing something to deal with your condition and they pity you less."

"I think he's right," Hiram said.

Around the table, heads nodded, but I had one more question for the group: "Did the fact I had deluded myself so badly devalue the Dispatches I'd drafted so much that we should just close up shop? Disband COPs Corner?"

"No," Del said. "You drafted the Dispatches but all of us discussed and agreed to the topics to be covered, and then we reviewed your draft and all of us agreed to the final version. Furthermore, I reviewed the six items in our creed. They are all good and true as far as I am concerned. Now these lessons Hiram,

Notso, Norb, and Oscar shared with us point to Creed Number Seven: Self-delusion is an insidious beast. Guard against it."

Oscar said, "Those examples show it could happen to any of us."

"Won't happen to me," Ollie said.

Skinny Norb replied, "That why you always buy clothes two sizes too small?"

We approved Creed Number Seven forthwith.

COP Creed:

1. The world is going to hell in a handbasket.
2. It is hell-bent-for-election to get there.
3. There IS something we can do about.
4. Find one opportunity to forgive an annoying dweeb every day.
5. COPs must watch The Oxbow Incident movie or read the book. Doing both is best.
6. Number Four above does not apply if the dweeb is packing a gun.
7. Self-delusion is an insidious beast. Guard against it.

Before we issued Dispatch Number Five, we discussed whether to use the Donald Trump example. Two of us did not want to mention him. Four of us did.

Ollie and Oscar were the pro-Trumpers.

We also debated whether we should adopt a policy of unanimous agreement on the content of a Dispatch before we send it.

"I had a tour in NATO," Norb said. "Unanimous approval means you never get anything done."

"Right," Del jumped in. "Even the angels couldn't get unanimous approval of how heaven and earth should work. And it got so heated in their discussion, God had to kick half the angels out of heaven."

"Look at the twenty-five-hundred-year history of Europe." Norb said. "It's a history of European nations fighting each other, one war right after the other. Aside from the US and Canada, the rest of NATO is European. Unanimous approval in NATO means European nations can't get into more wars with each other. It works for the alliance." He raised a finger.

"Another thing. The alliance does unanimously agree that Russia is a dangerous enemy. Defending Europe from the territorial predator to the east is the main reason NATO exists."

"Their raison d'etre," Del said.

"Great!" Ollie said. "Now he's talkin' dictionary."

I tried to get us back on course. "To this point in our history, unanimous approval hasn't been a problem for us. We all agreed to the content of our Dispatches, but then the issue of using a Trump example came up, and now we have differences of opinion. As Del pointed out, since creation, unanimous approval has been hard to come by at times.

"We need to remember what we're trying to do with our Dispatches, which is to bridge the chasm dividing Americans into hard-over, uncompromising camps. We are trying to change people's behavior, and we will have to deal with tough subjects to have a chance to accomplish our goal. To get there, we can't allow ourselves to get bogged down, or stopped dead in our tracks, if we have one dissenting voice. Majority rule should prevail."

"Agree," Hiram said. "Most formal organizations function on a majority rule policy."

Five Poops stared at their beers as if wondering if the contents of their glasses would still taste like beer. They took tentative sips, and unanimous little grins brightened their faces. I sipped my fizzy. I knew what it would taste like. It always tastes like stupid fizzy water.

We agreed then. Majority rule would rule the Poops.

After we launched Dispatch Number Five, responses poured in. Not one of them had a thing to do with the word "crippled," though. We did get a handful of responses giving Dispatches an atta-boy for digging out personal flaws, character defects, and stupid-headedness. The majority of the emails, though, had to do with us slinging mud at The Donald. Eighty percent of these responses castigated us mightily, at length, and in exceptionally clear and colorful language. These responses can be summarized as: "How dare we!!??," though in words weak, brief, and bland compared to the originals. Twenty percent of the respondents said words to the effect: "About time someone sniped at the egomaniac."

Four to one pro-Trump.

Among the founding Poops, we are two to one anti-The Donald.

"All right," Ollie said. "I stuck with the Poops through Dispatch Number Five, but in the next one, we have to treat President Trump with balance and respect. Otherwise, I'm quitting."

"Don't go away mad, Ollie," Norb said. "Just go away."

I jumped in. "Ollie, are you packin'?"

He looked indignant. "No."

"Norb," I said, "Creed Number Four applies here."

"Wait!" Ollie glared at me. "You calling me a dweeb?"

"No."

"You're not calling me one out loud is what you mean, isn't it?"

"No, Ollie," Norb said. "You are not a dweeb. Not out loud, or un-loud, or any other way. And I apologize for what I said. I was a dweeb to say what I did."

Ollie sat back; deer-in-the-headlights troweled over his jowly face. Before he could figure out what to say, Ted Tapman set a pitcher of beer on the table. And the glass of, you know. Our bartender was a specialist in just-in-time delivery.

Before he returned to the bar, Ted said, "You remember how you ended Dispatch Number One? You ought to make those three items the next element of your creed."

We unanimously agreed Ted was right. We also unanimously agreed we would not attribute the idea to our bartender.

The founding COPs believe we have adequately dealt with the word "crippled." There is, however, a broader consideration. The use of derogatory, demeaning, insulting, belittling terms to inflict mental suffering. As stated previously, a number of us founding COPs are crippled. That's how we think and talk about ourselves. But there is no intent to wound, to insult, to demean in our usage.

Not that long ago, the name "Karen" came to be an insult. Use of the name in that way was intended to cause anguish and suffering. "You're such a Karen," meant "You're such a dweeb."

Which inflicted more insult on every Karen on the planet than it did on the person intended to be insulted. This was certainly the case with the spouse of one founding member, whose spouse is named Karen.

The thing is, none of us founding COPs recall any expression of outrage or even annoyance at "You're such a Karen." Where were the political correctness police? Where were the woke? Aren't there already enough standard insults for the females among us?

Blonde means dumb. A woman's place is in the kitchen. Why wasn't there outrage over another insult named after a female? Why wasn't there insistence that, this time, a man's name be used to insult? You're such a Zephaniah! Like that.

The political correctness police and the woke probably thought the cruelty inherent in "You're such a Karen" was more than offset because it was new, clever, slightly outrageous, and old poops could be counted on to like it notso much.

We said at the outset, one of our purposes in launching Dispatches was to bridge the gaps separating the American populous into factions. To bridge these gaps between left and right, young and old, woke and un-woke, we need to do a number of things: listen more, curb the hair-trigger on our tongues, think, try to see the other side, and stop hurling insults.

If even a few of us manage to do these things on a regular basis, we will begin to build bridges instead of cursing the chasms.

New Subject.

After we launched Dispatch Number Four, we received more than one hundred requests to join COPs.

We were pleased.

Following the issuance of Number Five, 78.5% of the applicants withdrew their membership requests. All of the withdrawers were upset over our treatment of former president Trump. Within the founding COPs we had heated discussions as well. Among us founders, the reasoning behind our positions boiled down to these factors:

Anti-Trumpers were upset with him over how he handled COVID. He started out good. He declared war on the pandemic. It was, in one opinion expressed, the most presidential thing the man had ever done. But then time for reelection loomed, and the pro-gun, anti-abortion, close-the-borders, stop-printing-and-giving-away-money, and anti-maskers and -vaxers started shouting their messages. Saving American lives from a deadly disease, safeguarding our economy from the effects of combating the contagious virus weren't important. Reelection was all that mattered. Some of us could not forgive the Commander-in-Chief for that failure to do his duty in a war he declared. They became the anti-Trumpers among us.

The pro-Trumpers position was equally clear and straight forward: Nobody can martial support against the reprehensible far left than The Donald. Period. End of story. That's all she wrote.

In our country, we used to assemble ourselves into conservative and progressive, Republican and Democratic, and left and right camps. To get things done, people realized that perfect solutions for the left, and perfect solutions for the right were unobtainable. So, compromises were made. Now we assemble into far, far left and far, far right camps, where compromise is considered cowardice in front of the enemy and a firing-squad offense.

Even President Lincoln compromised. He said

words to the effect: If anything in this world is evil, slavery is. But he compromised with evil before the Civil War because to him, letting the union bust apart was a greater evil. The possibility of addressing that evil of slavery was better if the union held together. And the president was chastised by Frederick Douglass for the compromises he made to the slave states.

But the Civil War, and more than a hundred years of history since the Emancipation Proclamation, in the majority of the founding COPs opinions, proved President Lincoln right. The best path to meaningful emancipation lay with an intact union.

The fact that it took so long says something about we human beings. First, we are tribal beasts. Over many millennia, the instinct to band together for mutual protection, for survival was built into our DNA. Mutual protection wasn't just from saber-toothed tigers and cave bears. Many times, it was to protect my, our, tribe from their tribe. From that developed another set of bred-in notions: My tribe: good, good, good; Your tribe: bad, bad, bad. And from that, my tribe's ideas: good, good, good; their tribe's ideas: bad, bad, bad.

This evolutionary trait has inflicted a national lobotomy on American brains. We have far, far left brains and far, far right brains. Whatever is good, good, good for the far, far left, is bad, bad, bad for the far, far right.

We founding COPs recall the early seventies. Before he disgraced himself, President Nixon identified a Silent Majority abiding in our voting citizenry. To a probability of 82%, we founding COPs think he was right. Now, to an absolute certainty, there is no such thing. We do believe there is a puddle of silent voters who yearn for company in their lonely, quiet, centrist thinking. This puddle constitutes, perhaps, a mini-minority of the populace. The Founding Poops aim to give voice to this Silent Mini-minority.

In upcoming Dispatches, we will discuss Yellow Journalism and the internet. We have also added another book to our required reading list: Rules: A Short History of What We Live By, by Lorraine Daston. You'll be reading about that as well.

We close with a reminder of how we ended Dispatch Number One:

1. Stop shouting and listen.
2. Look for THE truth, not YOUR truth.
3. Work for balance in your outlook.

We amend these as:

1. Curb the hair triggers on our tongues. Stop shouting and listen. Think.
2. Try to see the other side. Look for THE truth, not YOUR truth.
3. Work for balance in your outlook. Do not hurl insults.

Till Dispatch Number Seven then, Notso Gentle Reader (And we wouldn't have you be any other way).

When I got to the Post, the other founding Poops were waiting for me. They pounced before I even ordered my stupid fizzy water.

"We have a real problem with the last two Dispatches," Hiram said.

"Yeah," from Norb. "They are real heavy Notso point of view. And almost nothing that looks or sounds like any of the rest of us founders."

"Wait," I said as I took my seat. "We meet. We discuss. We agree on topics. We agree on content. Every founding member's point of view is in everything we put in each and every Dispatch."

Ollie shook his head. Two of his three chins wobbled like balloons half-filled with water. "You discuss, and while we're trying to digest what you just said, you say, 'Next topic.'"

"Yeah," Oscar said. "It's like that Clint Eastwood cowboy show. *Head 'em up, move 'em out, keep them topics rollin'. Rawhide!* You stampede us into accepting what you got to say. Like that bit about President

Trump being derelict in his duty as Commander-in-Chief."

"Wait just a minute," I huffed. "Del said that."

"You told me that as we got close to the election," Del replied.

Oh! Then I remembered the discussion. We'd been talking about the Democrats and how they were trying to give stuff to people. We talked about how we saw America as providing opportunity for each person to make something of him, or herself, not have the government give stuff away to the masses. Without them having to work for what they got. By the sweat of your brow shall you earn your grits. We lamented the kind of people Americans would become if that requirement to work for your daily bread was no longer present.

Del and I agreed. Neither of us could vote for a Democrat. The Republicans offered another dose of Trump, and he was catering to the far, far right. They were equally repugnant to each of us. That's the point in our discussion when I lobbed in the bit about the C-in-C being derelict in his duty.

The realization gave me a pause on top of the pause I was already in. Previously, my inability to see my own faults gave me pause when I considered I was drafting material which would tell people where they were wrong and how they should mend their ways. Now I was having to admit to myself that my memory was suspect as well.

Who was I, such a flawed character, to tell others how to behave?

"Earth to Notso!"

I returned to earth and the American Legion Post.

"Jeopardy," Hiram said. "You push us to wrap up our discussions so you can get home in time for the 1630 TV show."

"Record the stupid program, why don't you?" Oscar growled.

"Jeopardy isn't stupid!"

"It's easy peasy, Notso," Norb said. "I can show you the app to download, and you can set up your TV to record the program from right here in the Legion Post."

"Norb, I'm not done talking to Oscar. Now you're trying to stampede me."

"Guys." Ted Tapman placed my fizzy on the table. "I recorded you guys." He punched a couple of spots on the phone and placed it on the table next to my drink.

And there we were. In living color. Spewing unadulterated snarkiness all over each other.

The recording ended. Ted picked up his phone and stuck it in his shirt pocket. He handed each of us a piece of paper. On the top half of the sheet was:

Member in Good Standing

Curmugeonly **O**ld **P**oop **Corner**

<u>Your Name Goes Here</u>

And the bottom half:

COP's CREED

1. The world is going to hell in a handbasket.
2. It is hell-bent-for-election to get there.
3. There IS something we can do about it.
4. Find one opportunity to forgive an annoying dweeb every day.
5. COPs must watch The Oxbow Incident movie or read the book. Doing both is best.
6. Number Four above does not apply if the dweeb is packing a gun.
7. Self-delusion is an insidious beast. Guard against it.

Ted headed for the door. All of us founding Poops watched him. Ollie's mouth hung open. Mine did too. I closed mine.

Hiram said, "I propose we accept Ted's notion and design of a membership card."

"All in favor?" from Oscar.

The Poops "Aye'd" the crap out of that proposal.

Del said, "I propose we make Ted another founding member."

"All in favor?" from Oscar again.

Ted, with his hand on the doorknob, jumped in, "You guys are *the* founding members. I am just a bystander."

"There is that," Norb said. "We could make Ted Member #1 and put "Founding Member" on our cards."

I shook my head. "Hold on. Del offered us a proposal. We need to vote on it, or table it, before we move on to something else. I vote we vote."

"All in favor?" Oscar, who else?

So, we voted to vote, and unanimously nay-ed Del's proposal. Then we agreed to the wording on Ted's membership card. He was "Bystander-in-good-standing. Ted Tapman."

We further agreed we needed to run our meetings according to a set of rules. Hiram volunteered to draft up such a set.

Rule Number One, unanimously approved, was that we'd begin each meeting with a reading of our COP Creed.

By that time it was 1600 and we hadn't even addressed the subject of our next dispatch and the book, *Rules, A Short History of What We Live By.*

I was not going to make it home for Jeopardy. So, I downloaded the stupid app. So, I downloaded the app, and set the TV up to record the program.

The other thing was, we'd all been so wrapped up in our discussion, no one had taken a head break.

One was needed. We all agreed to that.

Whilst in the room of relief and sometimes retreat, Norb said, "We're all here. We can continue to do Poop business."

Oscar said, "Norb! That was so grade school!"

"He's got a point though," Ollie said. "We didn't get much business done because we spent all afternoon dumping on Notso."

"I only have one proposal," Norb said. "That we take turns serving as chairman of our meetings."

"I shouldn't have a turn. You all thought I stampeded you into my way of thinking."

"Shut up, Notso." Del said. "Just agree with him."

Mr. All-in-Favor invited us to vote.

Unanimous approval, and the guys who'd already done their business got the heck out of Dodge.

Norb. Ever since he'd had the bout of COVID, his sensitivity to olfactory rudeness had disappeared. Notso the rest of us, however.

Ollie was the last to rejoin us at our table. He always was. "It's about dad-burned time," snuck through the unanimous smiley faces we wore. He and his fellow pro-Trumper, Oscar, were anti-vax and anti-mask. Ollie, however, had gone heavy-duty into the wash-your-hands bit. When he finished washing his hands, after using the facilities, he always left the water running until he dried his hands with a paper towel; then he used the towel as a special COVID shield to turn off the hot and cold water; then he used the paper towel to open the door; then he stood in the doorway and tossed the paper towel toward the waste basket. He never once hit the three-point shot.

The Post had a janitor service to square the place away after closing time, but Ted, when business at the bar permitted, policed up the heads. He got tired of picking up Ollie's towels, so, he kept a supply of plastic bags, that you get from stores these days, behind the bar, and he made Ollie tie a plastic bag to a belt loop to contain his used paper towels. That bag looked like it was a fourth chin, only there wasn't room for it up there under his real chin.

Hiram waited until Ollie plopped onto his chair. "While we waited for you, the rest of the group voted me in as chairman for the rest of today's meeting." Then he looked down at the three by five card on the table. "We will now discuss the book that Notso recommended to us: *Rules, A Short History of What We Live by*, by Lorraine Daston. Who wants to start?"

"What language was that book written in?" Oscar said.

"English," I huffed. "Obviously."

"Sure as shootin' wasn't 'Merican English," opined Norb.

"Got so I had to refer to a dictionary every other

word," Ollie said. "As I read, I even began to look up 'the' and 'a.'"

"The language was a bit high faluting," said Del. "It was a college professor writing to other college professors. William Faulkner wrote that way, too. But, I always found the effort to wade through his language was well worth it. I felt the same way about *Rules*."

"What do you think about that *Rules* book, Hiram?" Oscar said.

Hiram thumped his empty beer glass on the table. "First, you can call me Mr. Chairman."

"Well now," Ollie said. "I'll call you Mr. Look-at-me-I'm-as-important-as-all-get-out."

Del jumped in. "This is like the part in the *Rules* book where the author writes about the Rule of St. Benedict. A very lengthy set of very detailed rules guiding every aspect of daily monastery life, but more important than the rules themselves was the Abbot."

Ted placed a pitcher of beer on the table, and a you-know. "In the case of the COPs, your Abbot is the chairman."

"You read the book?" said Oscar.

Ted nodded.

Hiram raised his arm, ready to bang one of the bartender's principal pieces of equipment on the table again, when Ted grabbed his wrist, forestalling a shattered *gavel*. Ted took the fragile banger and placed it gently on the table. From the pocket in his apron, he pulled a tack hammer and five-inch section of two-by-four. "Use these, Mr. Chairman."

Ted Tapman, bartender extraordinaire, and Bystander-in-good-standing, guided us to COP meeting-conduct rules and respect for our chairman.

We finished our COP business, including a list of topics to be covered in the next Dispatch, in time to invite our wives to join us for Spaghetti Dinner Night at the Post. At the dinner, we had the best time, just being together.

And me, I felt relief. Most of the COP business that day was driven by the other COPs or Ted. I was off the hook for *raw-hiding* them into doing what I wanted them to do.

That night, lying in bed next to Jolene, My One and Only Squeeze, we counted the blessings God had bestowed on us that day and thanked Him for them. Then we prayed for all the people on our prayer list. Once you're in your eighties, that list is a long one. When we'd run through both our lists, we "Amen-ed" together.

Then she said, "George, you were … happy tonight. Ebullient even."

I decided to show her *ebullient* and laid a major lip-lock on her.

She pushed against my chest, and said, "Not tonight."

"Tomorrow, then?"

"Next year."

"I might not live that long."

"If we don't strain your heart, you might."

"If we don't strain my heart, I might not want to live."

"I want you to live."

Poop!

Oh well. One of the fringe bennies of living this long is that you get over that kind of disappointment quicker than you used to. That's the only thing you can do quicker.

A blessing, see?

Sort of.

Maybe.

Or not.

At any rate, I normally wake at 0500. The next morning, I got out of bed at 0400. I was anxious to get to drafting up the next Dispatch.

In this edition, we, the founding COPs, will be discussing *Rules, A Short History of What We Live by,* by Lorraine Daston.

We admit up front, that the majority of us founders found the language of this scholarly tome high faluting, pedantic, and off-putting. Del, however, pointed out that William Faulkner wrote stories using words drawn from the same intellectual stratum. He read most of that author's works with a dictionary to hand, and often, he'd finish a page, and then read it again with an understanding of the meaning of the words printed thereon.

Del said, "Sometimes a reader has to work as hard as the writer to dig out the ideas couched in language the author chose to use. And one man's pedantic is another's patois."

One of us Googled that word, and then we all agreed with Del.

And there were plenty of real gems to be mined from that *Rules* language if we worked to dig them out.

Hiram said, "I found the language of the book

difficult, but, in the end, I'm glad I plowed through it. It gave me an appreciation of the fact that animals have banded together for protection and to hunt more effectively since the fifth and sixth days of creation."

"To set the record straight," Oscar said, "I wasn't there at creation like Hiram was, but I can see now that fish school together, we have packs of hyenas, herds of elephants and murders of crows."

Murder of crows threatened to sidetrack our discussion, but our chairman kept us focused.

"I see the first humans banding together because they were tired of sleeping outside and running around naked, even in winter," Norb said. "They ganged up on a cave bear, stoned it, and appropriated its domicile, and everybody got a bear burger and a fur bikini."

Del said, "And we humans have evolved from cave-sized clans into cities, states, and nations. And the rules we live by have gotten more complex."

We founders discussed that topic at length. For the clan of the cave bear—a couple of us founders had read a book with that title—they only needed two rules:

1. No one is tough enough to take on a cave bear alone. If we band together, we get a place to live, something to eat, and clothes to wear.

2. If we band together, we need a leader. The biggest, toughest, meanest human stood up and thumped his chest and said, "I'm the leader." Like the old dog character in the *Aristocats* movie. If you argued with the leader, he would bop you on the bean

with an antediluvian Louisville Slugger and bite your ear off. He was the leader all right.

Nowadays however, our set of rules is considerably more extensive and complex. We even need a Supreme Court to sort out which side of an argument over the interpretation of a particular rule, or law, is the right one. Or the most right one. Or the one we are going to go with.

We founding COPs decided, unanimously, after some discussion, that we needed a set of rules to guide our conduct during our meetings. A set of such rules is now in place at COP Corner.

To remind, our objective in these Dispatches is to help us bridge the gaps that separate us into armed camps where our mouths become automatic weapons and we fire word bullets at each other across the no-man's, or -woman's, land between us. Each of us founders found, or discovered, if you prefer, that we had to examine our own behaviors, and in all cases, without exception, we had to amend our behaviors, and thought processes, before we could begin to suggest to others how they should examine their own consciences and find ways to activate the safety on their hair-trigger mouths.

Rules, to guide our lives, not just to put order into our meetings, we decided, were necessary to help us get there.

Hiram cited two examples from the *Rules* book. One was the Rule of St. Benedict. An extensive set of rules guided monastery monks' daily routines and behavior. But no matter how extensive the list of rules became, St. B. saw the need for an Abbot to rule an order and to have the authority to waive a particular rule in a particular situation if the Abbot deemed it appropriate to do so.

His second example cited the leaders in Paris centuries ago when they created a rule against people emptying their chamber pots from second story windows onto the streets and sidewalks below.

"Who could argue against that rule?" Hiram said. "According to the book, though, Parisians ignored the rule for a long time. I picture them parading about the streets with Dior poop parasols raised, sporting mid-calf boots and a clothespin on their noses. We founding Poops need to model our behavior on the Benedictine monks, not the Parisians."

When Hiram's last sentence was put forward as a proposal, we, the founding Poops were not unanimous in accepting the proposal as a rule, but the two dissenters did agree to abide by what the majority decided. So, it was decided.

Rules. Some of us can't accept some of them, but none of us can get along without them.

The last thing we did prior to issuing this dispatch was to review, and amend, our Creed.

COP's CREED

1. The world is going to hell in a handbasket.

2. It is hell-bent-for-election to get there.
3. There IS something we can do about.
4. Find one opportunity to forgive an annoying dweeb every day.
5. COPs must watch The Oxbow Incident movie or read the book. Doing both is best. *COPs must read *Rules, A Short History of What We Live by,* by Lorraine Daston.
6. Number Four above does not apply if the dweeb is packing a gun.
7. Self-delusion is an insidious beast. Guard against it.
8. *Before you tell others how to act, examine your own behavior. Do not go easy on yourself.

*New with this Dispatch.

When we founders got together again, we chose Oscar to serve as CFTD (Chairman For The Day). His first piece of business for us to consider was the membership card. Since we amended our Creed with the last Dispatch, did that mean we had to issue new cards to all the card-carrying members?

Besides the six of us who met in person, we were up to one-hundred-seventy online members. Email responses to our Facebook posts asked to join COP Corner. I had responded to the requests, printed out the membership cards on cardstock, and snail-mailed them to the new Poops.

Del proposed we issue the membership card with nothing on the back and post the current version of the Creed on our Facebook page. People could be encouraged to print the latest iteration and carry it in their wallets.

Since Oscar was also Mr. All-in-favor, he put the matter to a vote.

"Aye" rolled around the table like the ball on a roulette wheel.

"I'm glad to see that some of the people who un-joined Poops after we took a swipe at The Donald have rejoined," Norb said.

The CFTD sat at the head of the table with Ollie to his right. I sat at the foot and saw all heads turn and look at the pro-Trumpers.

Oscar shrugged. "Me and Ollie are glad, too."

"Notso," Del said, "We haven't heard much from you the last couple of meetings. What do you think about the matter?'

"Some of the pro-Donald types rejoining? I think that's good. Trump can inspire divisiveness. It feels better in this meeting that we can talk about the former president without any of us getting our skivvies twisted into a knot."

"Maybe we've grown up some," said Hiram.

"Not one of our wives would believe that."

"Neither would I." Ted placed a pitcher on the table.

"I propose we remove Ted's status as Bystander-in-good-standing," said Ollie.

We approved that proposal, and the CFTD asked Ted for his membership card.

Ted picked up the pitcher of beer and started to walk away. He left the stupid fizzy water.

"Wait a minute," Del said. "It's not a good idea to torque off the bartender. I propose we reinstate him."

That motion was approved, too, and we instated Ted a Bystander-in-real-good-standing.

The CFTD shook his head. "Guys, we ought to

be getting some business done here. Like what are going to write about in our next Dispatch. Anybody got any ideas?"

The sound of silence in our meeting room was silent-er than when Simon and Garfunkle sang about it.

After a pregnant pause, I said, "I've got an idea."

I proposed a topic. They ayed it. I thought about proposing that they designate me Founder-in-good-standing-again.

I kept my yap shut, though.

One of the things the COP Corner founders decided this past week was that our Creed consists of rules for ourselves. For anybody else who reads them, they are suggestions. If we tell you, you must change your behavior, unless you believe us, you will not mend your ways. More than likely, it will drive you further away from what we're trying to accomplish.

That means we have to trust you to listen to what we write, find objectivity in discerning its rightness or wrongfulness, and spend time in assaying the thoughts we present.

To the best of our ability, we will do that for you as well.

In this issue, we will suggest there is a general attitude towards our nation that we think needs to change. This attitude is critical of our nation and critical of its history. Things weren't perfect from its founding to the present, so it is inexcusably flawed.

During the Vietnam War, the same sort of attitude manifested itself in the younger generations of our nation. And in the opinion of the COP Corner founder Vietnam veterans, that attitude was more anti-America than anti-war. The attitude persisted through the eighties and only went away after Desert Storm. Now it is back. In spades. Bigger and *badder* than during Nam.

During Vietnam War time, there was protest against our involvement in the war. Some said we should worry about equal rights for all our citizens at home, not be involved in another foreign war. Others wanted free love and nickel baggies of pot.

Current left-ers want our government to do more for its underprivileged, victimized, marginalized minorities. The right-ers think the government is giving those same people too much, that they are really not victims automatically by virtue of race, gender, or creed, that if anyone is marginalized in our society it is the right-ers, that the government has already given so much money to its citizenry that no one wants to work anymore.

One of the things people seem to forget is that the Founding Fathers of our country did not promise us happiness. They promised the right to pursue happiness. To work for it, if you will. And if you are not happy, maybe the reason is not because it is not there to be had, maybe it's because you don't want to work for it.

Those who review the history of our country and find nothing but things to spark loathing and outrage should remember that our government is *rule of the people, by the people.* Whatever was wrong in the past, was wrong because of wrong people who rammed through wrong government.

In Exodus, God railed against "a stiff-necked people." There are plenty of examples throughout history, and in our own time, that our species has that proclivity. Parisiennes resisting the rule to not empty their chamber pots from second story windows onto streets and sidewalks, for example.

In our time, people resist more gun controls despite the number of young children who find unsecured handguns in the house and kill themselves or siblings. Then, of course, there's the school and mall shootings. This needless, senseless, widespread loss of life, from this one source, cries out for controls, rules, laws. And to curb this one wrong should not be that hard.

But we are a stiff-necked people. Many among us see enacting any new gun control laws as the first step to taking their precious weapons away from them completely. No one is seriously proposing that. Yet, we the people resist any curbs. The toddlers, the mall shoppers, the school kids, are they a small price to pay?

Bigotry, prejudice, hate crimes. These things exist today, and again, have abided in our species of animal since biblical times. Odds are these unsavory traits will constitute part of our spiritual makeup until the end of time, and we will have to deal with it until then. Right now, though, we stand on opposite sides of the street and hurl epithets across the center-striped pavement with enough animosity on both sides you have to wonder, are the bullets going to start flying soon?

The Chinese, the wetbacks, the Injuns, the Blacks are not ruining our nation. Erecting walls to keep all immigrants out is not the answer. We would not be a nation without them. Neither should we admit everyone. There are nations, religious powers who consider us evil and wish to do us harm. Fly planes into our skyscrapers. We need to find a middle road that bolsters the safety of our citizenry while admitting a number of those fleeing tyranny and a number of those, like Vietnam and Afghanistan, where we fought in a war we didn't know how to win and just quit and went home and abandoned those who had aligned with us during the fight, but now were left to face a hostile, vengeful majority.

No, it is not other races, nationalities, creeds ruining our nation. It is we the people who ruin it. Solutions to our problems require us to listen to each side of a matter. Both sides have legitimate concerns. The solution to our problems lies in taking stock of both sides' issues, finding a reasonable middle path that gives both sides a good bit of what they are looking for. Making things better than they are now. For both sides.

Most of us Poops grew up thinking the US of A was not only great, but the best country on earth. We believed that the documents drafted by our Founding Fathers were a more noble statement of what we as a people, we as a nation, were all about than any other such statement on earth. We believed it through all the protests in the 1960s and 70s. A lot of other people did too. President Nixon opined there was a silent majority in our nation. It seems to us that he may have been wrong about some things, but he was right about that.

We, the founding COPs, believe today that our country is the best one on earth. We have altered our belief somewhat from what we held growing up. The documents drafted by the Founding Fathers are not a statement of who we are, but who we can be. Those documents lay out who and what we as a nation can be if we work at it. That's what we believe, but we are not going to shout it to, or at you. We whisper it. And you can only hear it if you shut your yap and listen.

One last topic: the history of our nation.

WE COPs believe the history of our nation is replete with examples of things in which Americans can and should take pride.

In 2018, Norb Peabody, one of the COP founders, and his wife, took a trip to France which included a visit to Normandy. There they encountered groups of French school children touring the area as well. Norb reported being surprised to find young kids being taught to appreciate a key piece of their history. A piece, without which, the French nation would not have survived. He was also surprised to find the people around Normandy seemed appreciative of Americans and their contributions to winning World War II.

After he returned to the States, he told the rest of

us Wednesday-lunch-at-the-American-Legion-two-beers-only guys—we hadn't founded COPs yet—about his trip, and he said it also reminded him of: "Mr. Gorbachev, tear down this wall!"

Two instances where particular nations fostered coercive forms of ruling so repugnant that war became necessary to prevent them occupying more of the planet on which we live. Through the efforts of American military and American leadership, both aforementioned forms of government collapsed.

Not insignificant accomplishments. Pride-worthy even.

One-hundred-two years ago, American women received the right to vote in our country. Should they have received this inalienable right sooner? Should they not have had to fight so hard for it?

Looking back on it with twenty-first century wisdom, we Poops say, "Yeah verily." That it did not happen sooner, that it did not happen without a struggle, we lay that at the feet of the half of us humans who did not want to see it that way. We were Hu-mans, not Hu-womans. But the seeds of this form of equality were there in the founding documents. Plus, there was enough freedom there for the Hu-women to wage their struggle. They worked for it and won it.

We Poops admire American women for their struggle and victory.

And we admire our nation for giving them the wherewithal to get there.

It took a while, not because the nation was flawed, but because we citizens were a stiff-necked people.

And we Poops admire our nation for its women citizens' victory and making of our country a more perfect union.

A personal perspective:

The US Navy sent me, Gregory George Notso Normal, to Meridian, Mississippi, in 1968 for basic jet training. While my family and I were there, the KKK was in the midst of a campaign of violence. A Jewish synagogue was dynamited. For the two years before we arrived, every month, in the counties around Meridian, a Negro church was burned. Just before we arrived, shotguns blew out the front windows of two Civil Rights activists in town.

Most of the basic jet students were not married and lived in the Bachelor Officers Quarters on base. We married students rented houses in town. The day we moved in, the Welcome Wagon Lady called on us. She was very nicely turned out, with a hat and white gloves, and she was warm and welcoming.

I told her what I had seen in the paper and asked her if my family was safe there.

She replied, "Oh, yes, our Colored People know their place."

I said, "It's not the colored people I'm worried about. They aren't burning down their own churches."

She became the unwelcome wagon lady and took her leave posthaste.

One hundred five years after the Emancipation Proclamation, welcome to Meridian.

In 2010, I self-published a novel about an ensign during the early Vietnam War years who ran afoul of anti-war protestors. He disagreed with their philosophy and their protest and became inspired to apply for flight training.

My second novel, I decided would be about this same character arriving in Meridian. I finished a draft of this story in 2011 and decided I needed a research trip to the town. There I went to the library and perused copies of the town newspaper, *The Meridian Star*, from 1968.

One of the things I particularly wanted to read about was the time immediately following the Dr. Martin Luther King, Jr. assassination. I wasn't sure I had remembered one particular volume of *The Star*. But I had. It said a reporter had asked the Chief of Police if he expected any unrest because of the assassination. He said he did not. That he had given his officers shoot to kill orders. There had been no unrest, nor a single peep of protest.

After frying my brain reading microfiche for hours, I left the library to feed my eyeballs. Outside, I cranked up the engine of my pickup as two teenaged Black males sauntered down the sidewalk. They wore slung-low pants and earpieces and carried iPods. They were shucking and jiving to the tunes. After just immersing myself in 1968, this was a HOLY CRAP moment for me. A few blocks away, I entered a McDonalds and saw Black and white men sitting and eating together. HOLY CRAP moment *part deux*. After having lived in Meridian in 1968, having just relived that time through microfiche newspaper stories, this was an amazing sight. It was like, finally, President Lincoln's proclamation meant something. It took almost one-hundred-fifty years, but now, it meant something. And I saw that it did in a McDonalds.

A lot of people died to gain that progress. Civil War soldiers, Abolitionists. Black and white activists.

And are conditions perfect now? Most certainly not. But, they are better enough that there should be a lot of appreciation for what's been done. That doesn't mean stop trying to make things better, but it does mean that somewhere in a person's heart there should abide appreciation for what's been done by the people of this country. And we suggest, a bit of pride in what the blood sweat and tears of so many has accomplished would not be misplaced.

As a matter of fact, we founding Poops believe we don't need to make our country great again. It never stopped being great. What we the people need to do is to believe our country is, at this moment—great.

I, Gregory George Notso Normal, was one pooped puppy. It was 1910, you know, seven-ten p.m., Friday evening. I'd just hit "send" on Dispatch #8. This one sucked all the juice out of me. It was the hardest to get out. We went through God only knows how many rewrites and edits. Plus, it was the longest Dispatch by far.

I'd just sat down in front of the TV intending to watch a recorded episode of *Gunsmoke* when that *longest dispatch* thought niggled at me. I pushed myself up, groaning, and went back upstairs to my boy room and checked.

Wrong. #8 was seven pages long and so was #5. All the rest were four pages or less.

Okay already! Now we got that settled, can we go watch Gunsmoke *already?*

I figured Dispatch #8 would torque off the MAGA guys as well as the hard lefters. We Founding Poops would be standing in the middle of the street with both sides waving their signs and shouting at us at decibel levels above the threshold of pain. Just thinking about it was above the threshold of pain.

We'd talked about this extensively before we agreed to launch. We'd acknowledged that what we said would infuriate both sides, but we had to send it. The things we said were true to the best of our ability to define that squishy commodity.

Besides, Norb had said, "If we get both sides mad at us, maybe they'll talk to each other."

Snowball's chance in hell, is what I thought.

Del said, "Snowball's chance," and then, "Look. We knew we were going to get to this point shortly after we started *Dispatches*. We knew we couldn't get to where we're trying to go without going through this very spot. Both sides in their uncompromising zealotry need to be made to see that their close-mindedness is the problem. I don't see how we can do that without making them mad. We have to launch #8."

He convinced all of us, including me.

That was then. This is now, and I feel like I am the only one standing in the middle of the street with both sides aiming weapons at me.

An evil spirit minion of the devil reached clawed fingers out of the black pit of despair and grabbed me by the ankles and tried to pull me in. If I let him get me in there, I would be lost forever.

The first time I felt like this was when I was in my first semester of the second year of college. Jolene and I had been going steady for five years. Through US Navy boot camp, through electronics technician school, an assignment to a destroyer, and then through a year and a half in college, she'd stuck with me. All around me, guys received "Dear John" letters from their hometown girlfriends. Up to the start of my sophomore year, Jolene and I were good. I'd made third-class petty officer before starting at Purdue. I told her if I made second class, which I was up for in the next semester, I could afford for us to get married.

I thought she'd be pleased to have something solid in front of us to look forward to.

"What if you don't make second class?" she'd said.

Then she'd said, "I think we both should date other people. To be sure about each other."

That was an icicle through my heart. I'd called her from the phone in our upstairs set of rooms me and three of my navy buds, all on the same college program I was, rented from this widow lady. I was sure I knew it was a prelude to a "Dear John." Jolene didn't want to sledgehammer me with it. She wanted it to sneak up on me.

I hadn't planned on going home next weekend. I basically could afford to drive the six hours, one way, once a month. And I'd just been with her Friday night, Saturday, and Sunday. She hadn't said a peep to my face about dating other guys. No. The message came over the phone.

This was not good. I had to go home.

The next weekend, as I drove through Illinois, the highway conveyed me through a railway underpass. Concrete pillars supported the elevated rails. *Just drive into a pillar.* At seventy MPH. It'll be over in a flash, rather than living in agony the rest of my life without Jolene.

Something kept me on the road, though. I couldn't see Jolene on Friday. She was on a date with someone else. She was a student in nurse's training. I was sure she was out with a med school dude. Her mother pushed her in that direction. *Why would you want to be a nurse unless it was to snag a doctor?* The woman I wanted to be my mother-in-law was not on my side.

Saturday morning, I went to a jewelry store and priced out an engagement ring of the kind Jolene wanted. Not a round one. An emerald cut. A half carat was half what my new Plymouth Valiant was worth. And I owed Mom and Pop for half of that already.

I could go on with this for pages yet, but suffice it to say, Jolene dated a few more guys. I dated two girls. One time each. With the second one, I wound up with her tongue in my mouth. *Gag!*

Of course, after Jolene and I had been married a while—I guess I don't need to go into that either.

We both decided we'd had enough dating others to know we were meant for each other.

Now, the second time I stood next to the gaping maw of the pit of despair, I was a US Navy captain and the commanding officer of an amphibious ship. By that time, I'd been in the nav for twenty-five years. To that point, I'd never really decided to be a career sailor. Good jobs just kept popping up for me. Thank You, God

Right after I took over, and my boss, a senior surface-navy captain, showed me around my ship and pointed out things I should get fixed chop-chop. The things he was concerned with were appearance things. I knew we had major problems in the engineering spaces. The out-going commanding officer had told me about them, and the chief engineer had showed me rusted, leaky fuel pipes in the bilges of the engine room. A major safety hazard.

I said, "I've got something I'd like to show you, Captain."

So, I led him down to the leaking fuel pipes.

He said, "You're a goddamned aviator. What do you know about ships? I'll tell you. Not one damned thing. By the time I come back again, you better have taken care of the items I pointed out to you topside."

He glared at me, and I glared back. "I heard you surface navy types were all form over substance."

A surprise mask supplanted his mad one. He looked like I'd slapped him. Then the now-I'm-really-mad mask settled into place. He turned and stomped away and up the ladders to the main deck.

I stayed there looking down at my rusty fuel pipes thinking, *Well Gregory George Notso—I'd been Notso since I was a junior lieutenant—you've just stepped into a bucket—no a fifty-five gallon drum—of feces!*

Like I said, I'd never really thought about making the navy a career. I just took the jobs one at a time. But at that moment, I really did think I *really* did want the chance at the next job. I just might be able to snag command of an aircraft carrier. But I'd just blown that big time by telling my boss he was a stuffed-shirt, head-up-his-butt dipwad.

So, I stood there staring into the bilges, and the rusty pipes faded, and I beheld this pit at my feet, which extended all the way to hell, and a devil-minion grabbed my ankles, and he tried to pull me in.

I prayed: *Father God, Who art in heaven, protect us Stoopids from our own dumb selves.*

He heard me. I wound up with the ship with the best appearance in my boss' unit, and with a sound engineering plant as well. And, thank You, God, I wound up commanding an aircraft carrier.

For crap sakes, Notso. Get your stuff together. You're doing all this to avoid thinking about Dispatch #8. You're scared of what the reaction is going to be.

The above was all about me, but I showed it to the Founding Poops, and they agreed I should leave it in the history. They had all worried that dispatch would unleash a holy hell of backlash.

"Ted might not even serve us," Hiram said as we sat at our table at a rare Saturday meeting of the Founding Poops.

Ted served us, with, "Condemned Poops' last pitcher."

Then he smiled, and we all relaxed thinking he'd just been kidding. We hoped like heck he'd been kidding.

Ted Tapman had not been kidding.

Hiram Mudd was our CFTD (Chairman For The

Day). Owl Ohlenschlager, the American Legion post commander, dragged a folding chair to the head of our table and told Hiram to move over some and plopped his ample butt—it looked like he'd *floofed* out his tail feathers before he sat—on the chair.

The Post Commander plunked a heavy crystal beer mug on the table. PC, in big gold letters on the side opposite the handle, proclaimed his status. He filled his mug from our pitcher and drank. Owl's Adam's apple poked out of his turkey neck. It bobbled up and down, up and down. Replunking his half-empty mug, he looked up and scowled. His fierce eyes circumnavigated the table and lasered, for a long moment, each of us Poops.

"Finish your beer. Then get out. You are no longer members of this post."

I sat opposite the PC. He really did look like a hooter. Chin strap whiskers framed his round flat face implanted with big, yellowish-brown eyeballs. Those dispassionate orbs regarded us, as if we were mice and he was trying to decide if he was hungry, or if it would be fun to just kill us. His little beak of a nose jutted out of pasty complected … face feathers?

Hiram said, "Our meeting hasn't come to order yet."

"And it ain't gonna," The PC hooted. "It's over before it even started. I didn't come over here to argue this with you. Clear out. Now."

"I'm a paid-up life member," Del said. "I'm not leaving.

"We're all paid up members," the CFTD said. "And it is not in the bylaws that the PC can arbitrarily kick members out. None of us are leaving."

"Who do you think you are? Who do you think you're talking to? Who—"

That's when Norb dumped the rest of the pitcher in Owl's lap.

The PC jumped up. His chair fell over behind him. He looked down at his sopping crotch and shook his head. The eyes, now blazing with the cold fire of homicide, came up again.

"You ain't heard the last of this."

"Right now, Owl," Oscar said, "I bet you're wishing you were a duck."

"Yeah," said Ollie. "We could even make a new saying: Like beer off a duck's belly."

"We should bring a duck in here and try it out," Oscar said. "You know. To see if beer really will run off its belly."

Owl's face turned red, then morphed into purple.

"Hell hath no fury," Norb said, "like that of a purple-faced, pissed off, post commander."

The PC spun around, stumbled when he kicked the folding chair, and, with one foot stomping and the other leg limping, he exited through the meeting room door.

"Don't go away mad," Hiram said.

Oscar piped in with, "Yeah, just go—"

The CFTD banged the hammer on the two-by-four section. "Order. Come to order."

I stuck my hand up. CFTD nodded.

I said, "Owl is temporary PC. He only got the job because nobody else wanted it after Ward Band had the stroke. He's only got the job for another two weeks."

"Right," Hiram said. "He's a lame duck CP."

The hammer banged the table again. "Knock it off. And come to order. No more BS-ing!"

"Mr. Chairman." Ted placed a full pitcher on the table.

CFTD Ollie nodded.

"My wife Sybil and Owl's Mabel are good friends. Mabel told her that her two college grandkids complained to Owl about your last Dispatch. 'Blame the victims. That's what all you Neanderthals do.' Owl didn't want his grandkids thinking he was a Neanderthal. That's what Mabel said."

"Any of the other Post members complain about the Dispatch?" Del said.

Ted: "Yeah. Eight guys wanted you banned from here for the rest of the year. For badmouthing Trump."

"Like, put on time out?" Del again.

"Owl said he'd do that one better. Boot you Neanderthals out for good." Ted looked down at the puddle on the floor. "That's beer, right? Owl didn't pee his pants, did he?"

CFTD said, "It's beer."

Ted said, "I'll clean it up then."

Norb, though, volunteered to do it. I, Gregory George Notso Normal, got up to help him.

CFTD said, "Notso, sit." Ollie sucked in a big lungful and huffed it out. "You wanted this emergency meeting. The rest of us thought we should let things sit over the weekend. See if this thing blows over."

"Yeah." I shook my head. "None of the rest of you got personal threats by personal email." I scowled. "I'm thinking we should pull the plug on COP Corner. Just let it fade away into the sunset. We could go back to being Wednesday-lunch-at-the-American-Legion-two-beers-only guys."

Del stuck up his hand. CFTD nodded *you have the floor.* "I propose we do not throw in the towel on COP Corner or our Dispatches."

"Second the motion." Norb from his hands and knees.

Mr. All-in-favor Oscar said what he says in situations like we had then.

"Point of order, Mr. Chairman," I said. "We need to discuss this before we vote.

"There were probably a thousand responses to Dispatch #8. We were called Neanderthals, troglodytes, *nutsos*, plus a plethora of pure profanity. Plus, we—I—was/were banned from Facebook. Plus, I got personal threats, and a personal threat to me threatens Jolene as well."

"I already said, 'All in favor'."

"Yes, Oscar, I know. But in this case, we do need a bit of discussion before we vote."

Del stuck up his hand.

Chairman nod.

"We knew we were going to draw some flak. So, we've drawn some."

"*Some* flak!" I said. "I never saw this much flak over downtown Hanoi."

"You're out of order, Notso. Furthermore, we know what you think. We need to hear from the others. So, I'm going to poll the rest of you. Ollie?"

"Del's right. We knew we'd catch flak. So, we did, but I think we should let things ride over the weekend and get together Tuesday and figure out what to do next. But I do not want to throw in the towel. Hell, I think we should say, 'We have not yet begun to fight'."

"Oscar."

"Del'n Ollie are right. All-in-fav—"

The hammer-gavel banged.

"Norb, anything else you want to say?"

"Not me, Mr. chairman."

"Now, Oscar."

"All in fav—"

"Hold on," I said. "Exactly what proposal are we voting on?"

"That we not disband COP Corner nor quit the Dispatches. Oscar."

"All in favor."

"Aye," x 5. Against one stinkin', puny, pipsqueak nay.

CFTD said, "The ayes have it. Do I have a motion to adjourn?"

"One other piece of business, if you please, Mr. Chairman?"

A nod to Norb.

"I propose everybody get a copy of *The Age of Acrimony*. I further propose everybody read it, and next week, we can vote on whether to add it to our required reading list."

Nod.

"All in favor?"

"Aye," x 6.

Then Del said, "I propose we send out another Dispatch. Today. A simple one. We can vote on it before we adjourn."

This emergency meeting sure didn't go like I wanted. I considered getting in my pickup and finding a concrete pillar to drive into. Actually, the thought flitted through my head, but I didn't think it. It thunk itself.

The Five, that's how I was thinking of them, liked Del's proposal. I didn't. I had wanted to quit. I'd backed off from that, but I still wanted to hunker down and let a little of the heat blow over.

The Five, though, they were all like *In your face, Dude!*

Del said he'd establish a COP Corner Twitter page and would send out the next dispatch.

Ollie had one last proposal: That Gregory George odd-man-out Notso Normal be reclassified as "Member in-less-good-standing than Ted Tapman."

We have not yet begun to fight.

Saturday was one of those nights. Sleep would not happen. Sleep wasn't even close. Actually, it was just on the other side of the bed. Jolene slept. Even without my hearing aids, I could hear her breathing. In. Out. *Inn. Ouout. Innn. Ououout.*

Such a peaceful, restful sound. A quiet sound. It barely made a ripple on the surface of the silence of the night. Silence and the deep, dark night. Night kept the light away. Night was the time for sleeping. In. Out. In. Out.

I tried to take in some of Jolene's surrender to the silence.

Soporific silence. Thinking of silence as sleep-inducing. Maybe that would help.

Silence surrounded me. I heard it out there. It was weighty and above me and pressed me deeper into my soft Sleep Number Bed set at twenty. Beneath me, the airbag in my side of the bed was filled with it. It was to the sides of me. I felt it hovering just outside my ears.

But the bloody, stinkin', stupid silence! Would it

slither into my ears and take up residence inside my head and push the clamorous, loud, insistent voices out and help me get to sleep?!

Simon and Garfunkle, where the crap are you?! I need you guys, you know?

Those—not S & G—voices kept yammering: *Fairweather friend!; The going got tough, and you got going!; The enemy started shooting, and you ran away!; Desertion in the face of the enemy! Coward! Traitor!*

The soundtrack played inside my box-of-rocks brain; then it kicked back to the start and auto-played all over again. And again. And again. And again. Ad nauseam!

I felt sick to my stomach.

Do not puke! If I puked next to the bed, Jolene would—

Throwing the covers back, I swung my legs over the side.

Don't look at the clock.

But did I listen to myself? I did not. Midnight thirty. Oh dark thirty.

Father God in heaven! Morning was a gazillion light-years away. Night and silence had become my enemy.

Well. At least I could do something useful. Wake up in the middle of the night, what do you do? I headed for my bathroom, the one at the other side of the house. The one off our bedroom had become Jolene's.

Barefooted, skivvy drawered, I padded past the

mostly glass front door. And stopped. On the far side of our circle sat a pickup truck. Beyond the circle, at the four-way-stop intersection, another pickup turned toward our house and doused its lights.

Those guys who'd sent the email threats were coming for me! And, worse, Jolene!!

I hustled downstairs and got my pump sixteen gauge. The shells I kept in a firesafe which held important papers and the shotgun shells.

Hurry the crap up!

The stupid combination kept getting itself screwed up. *Finally!*

Jam five shells into the under-barrel magazine and grab extra shells to put in my pocket.

Stoopid! You ain't wearing no pants. You're in your skivvies! Stupid, all right!

Leaving the safe open and a few dropped shells on the floor, I hustled back upstairs and looked out the front door. Only one pickup? I expected to find two.

The back of the house!

I hustled to the kitchen and flipped on the switches for the backyard floodlights. Nobody there. Nothing moved. *Back to the front door!*

Wait. Is that Hiram's pickup on the far side of our circle? Sure looks like it.

I opened the front door and stepped out onto the stoop, intending to see what Hiram was doing there.

The door of the pickup flew open, and a big guy jumped out.

Not Hiram! I thought. My heart inhaled a slug

of thirty-degree Fahrenheit blood. I pumped a shell into the chamber and off-ed the safety.

"Notso! It's me! Hiram!"

Sweet Jesus! I safed the gun.

Just as Hiram neared, the front door opened behind me.

Jolene said, "Gregory George Normal! What are you doing standing on our front porch in your underwear?? And holding a shotgun?!"

That's when we heard the sirens. In the distance. But as we listened, they got closer.

Jolene shook her head. "Now what?!"

"G. George!" Jolene had this drill sergeant voice that she used now and then. "Put some pants on and put that stupid gun away. In that order."

I would have said, "Yes, Dear," but I feared it would take too much time.

In the bedroom, I grabbed my jeans and had one leg on when the sirens sounded close enough that a police car was likely to bust through the windows and run me over. I kind of hop-walked back to the front door. Like Marshall Dillon's stiff-legged deputy Chester moves when he's in a hurry.

Jolene and Hiram stood side-by-side looking out our closed front door.

"Five, six," Jolene said. "Six police cars! What in the world did you ... you *men* do?!"

Four of the lights-blazing-and-sirens-blaring-for-all-getout cars turned into the circle up the hill from ours. Hector's circle.

The second last police car swerved into our circle and stopped by Hiram's pickup. He'd left the driver-side door open and the dome light glaring. Cops notice stuff like that.

A cop bolted out both front doors of their car and approached the pickup with guns drawn.

The last car in line stopped on our side of the circle. Two policemen boiled out of the car, drew their handguns, and following the flashlights they held in the other hand, hustled toward the backyard between our house and Hector's.

"Sh—," Hiram said, "oot!"

"What did you do?" the DI really wanted to know.

"Well," Hiram said, "Notso got these email threats after he posted our last dispatch."

Jolene's eyes gored me.

"I didn't tell you because I didn't want to worry you."

"Next time, worry me!!"

"When Notso told the five of us about the threats he received, we poked fun at him for being worried. But later on, Del set up a conference call. Talking it over, we decided we shouldn't just blow off those threats. We set up a watch list to keep an eye on the front of your house. Del put on a Ghillie, a camouflage suit SEAL snipers use, and he's watching the back."

"Good Lord!" Jolene said. "The police could shoot him!!" She looked at me. "Finish putting on your damn pants!!"

Jolene said damn!!

She flipped on the front porch light, pulled open the door, and stepped out.

The sirens had quit, but from up the hill, a lot of dogs were barking up a storm.

The two officers by Hiram's truck were staring in that direction.

"Officers!" Jolene called.

They looked. She beckoned. They aimed their flashlights at her and started toward her.

I took a step towards the door, but Hiram grabbed my arm. "Your pants."

The officers' flashlight beams hit us in the open doorway.

"Don't anybody move!"

Jolene had her hands in front of her face shielding her eyes. She didn't move. Hiram stood statue still.

"You there. Finish putting on your damn pants!"

It was pretty clear to whom they were talking. So, I moved. I got my other leg in the jeans. I even remembered to pull up the zipper.

Then Jolene explained about Del watching the back of the house.

"That's what started this ruckus," Blond Crewcut Officer said. "Your neighbor looked out his back window and saw a man's face lit up by a cell phone. The man appeared to be sneaking up on his house, and he called 911."

"He wasn't sneaking up on anybody's house," Hiram said. "Del was just using the brush behind that house to hide in as he watched the rear of the

Normal's house. Mr. Normal here got some email threats that worried us. We were just trying to make sure he and his wife didn't get hurt."

The other officer had Elvis-hair. He spoke over his radio. Then he said, "Ma'am, can we come in and get some statements from you all?"

She agreed and put on a robe and a pot of coffee. In that order. The two officers, Hiram, and I sat around our kitchen table.

"Okay," blond crew-cut officer said, "One of you tell us what happened to cause this … mess."

"Well, officer," Hiram said. "It's this way."

"Wait!" Elvis Hair officer said. "COP Corner. You're the guy who tumbled ass—. The guy who did the somersault in his front yard the day after you guys posted about balance on Facebook."

Jolene placed mugs in front of the officers and poured for them. She looked at me. "Milk and sweetener."

I followed orders as she took a seat and began a cogent, concise, crisp *Reader's Digest* condensed version of the events leading up to the excitement that night. As she spoke, I poured coffee for Hiram and myself. There was a pretty dim prospect of getting any sleep that night. Damn the caffeine! Full speed ahead! Whatever.

Jolene finished her dissertation.

Elvis Hair rose and walked back outside. Pretty clear what he was doing. Radioing in what he'd learned.

A couple of minutes later, Elvis Hair returned.

"Ma'am, the chief says he'd like you to come to the station Monday morning and sign a statement. It'll be a transcript of what we recorded you saying. You agree to that?"

She did.

"You Curmudgeonly Old Poops, however. Chief wants you to come with us to the station *now* for questioning."

Hiram and I went with them. In separate cars. Mine was like a big dog cage in back. Big enough for me to sit with my feet with feet up on the seat and a Great Dane standing. *Just a few minutes ago, it seemed like not being able to get to sleep was the worst thing!*

At the station, they led me into an interrogation room and left me there by myself. They let me stew in the hot anguish of waiting and wondering *What the crap is coming next?*

Time lazy-snail-ed along. I had no watch or cell phone. No clock on the wall. My tiny cube didn't have one of those one-way windows like the interrogation room on *NCIS*. I wouldn't have minded if Leroy Jethro Gibbs came in, looked me in the eye, and said, "Spill your guts, or I will ram my hand down your throat, rip your heart out, and squeeze it bone dry in front of your face before your eyes go dim."

Now Leroy would have never said that to me. I'm his biggest fan. Anyway, it wasn't Gibbs who finally jerked open the door behind me and kicked my heart into high gear. Officer Wyechewski, by his nametag, butt-slammed himself onto the chair across from me.

Chewey glared. By that time, with all the waiting, I was torqued off some, and I glared right back at him.

After a long, double-sided glower, Chewey said, "Knock it off with the stare down!"

"You started it!"

Chewey rolled his eyes. "Just goddamn tell me what goddamned happened!"

He had a laptop open in front of him, and as I started telling, he pointed it at me. It turned out he had a dictation app. When I finished talking, he said, "Wait here."

Cop humor. He let himself out with a key. I obviously was not provided one.

Long minutes later, he returned with a printout of my statement. I started reading it and stopped. "This is replete with misprints, punctuation errors, and spelling mistakes. I'm not signing this!"

Back to the double-sided glower.

"Let me use your stupid laptop. I'll fix the typos." I wiped off my glower. "Can I use your stupid laptop, please?"

I could. I un-typo-ed it. He printed it. I signed it.

"Now, get the—insert naughty word—out of here."

"You gonna' give me a ride home?"

"Walk!"

I smiled. "I can see it now. The headline of our

next post on Twitter: How the city police treated an eighty-one-year-old victim."

He unloaded on me then. He'd been on call, but sleeping peacefully he was, when he gets the call. And for what? A half dozen crazy old farts—

"Not farts," I interjected. "Poops."

It was pretty clear *that* cop was not happy with *the* COPs. Actually, none of the city or county cops were happy with us COPs. Then Chewey put me in an Uber, and said, "The city'll pay for it but bill you later."

The driver pulled into my driveway at 0515 by his dashboard clock, stopped, and half-turned in his seat. "The city doesn't tip us. How about it?"

"You want a tip? Here's one. When you give a guy a ride home from the police station, don't ask him for a tip!"

I opened the door, and with one leg out, my conscience stopped me. I'd forgotten I had one. "Wait," I said. Jolene had reminded me to take a key. I entered the house, returned with my wallet, and handed him some bills. "Thanks for the lift. It would have been a heck of a walk without my cane."

Back inside, I found Jolene on the living room sofa next to the table lamp connected to a timer that turns the lamp on at sunset and off at rise. She had her lectionary open.

Oh yeah. Sunday.

She would be the lector for nine o'clock Mass. The lectionary tells her how to deliver the readings.

"You coming back to bed?" she said.

Normally, I am up by five a.m. I shook my head.

"Wake me at six-thirty."

She closed her book and rose. When we have the lamp on the timer, it is set to dim. When she reads there, she turns the lamp up to high. She didn't turn it back to dim. *Think of all the electricity you'll waste.* I almost said that.

Instead: "Sweetheart, I'm sorry I disturbed your beauty sleep."

"Your friends were worried about us."

"So, you're not mad?"

"Not at them."

Oh!

She went to bed. I entered the kitchen to turn out the backyard floods, but before I did, I noticed lights on at Hector's house. They have a family room in back. It looked to be full of people.

I unplugged my cell from the charging cord and texted Hector.

"U OK?"

He emoji-ed a thumbs up and "U?"

Text: "Yah. Just got home from police station."

Text: "Come up."

I checked on Jolene. In. Out. In. Out.

Text: "On the way."

Hector was hosting a gathering of the up-the-hill neighbors. They wanted to know my side of the story. They offered me breakfast wine. I accepted a fizzy water and told them what I knew.

"What about your Poop buddies?" Hector wanted to know.

"They kept us separated. I'll text them and see if any respond."

Hiram responded. He'd signed a statement. They released him but told him the city and county would bill us for the 911 call response.

Norb and Ollie responded with basically the same message. Del and Oscar did not reply. That was worrisome.

"Look," I said to the neighbors, "I'm sorry us COPs caused such an unholy fiasco last night. If I had known they were doing this, I'd have warned you, Hector."

"I know. And quite frankly, most of us were following your posts, and we saw the threats and nasty responses to the last one. All of us support what you're doing."

"Thanks. And again, sorry."

"Be notso worried, Notso," up-the-hill Arnold said. "Most excitement we've had here since we moved in twenty-seven years ago. Heck, even Hector's rotgut vino tastes like ambrosia with a little excitement chaser."

Then I left to roust Jolene out of bed.

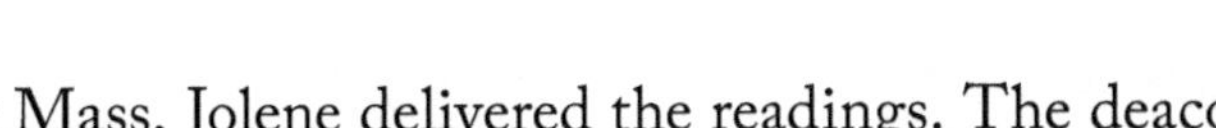

At Mass, Jolene delivered the readings. The deacon read the gospel. Father Ed delivered the sermon.

During that, Jolene elbowed me in the ribs eleven times.

After Mass, I texted Del. He called right back. He and Oscar had just been released. He'd spoken with the others, and they were meeting at the Legion Post for lunch. With their wives.

"Can you and Jolene join us?"

I explained what Del said.

"Speaker," DI-voice said.

Carefully, I punched the right hotspot on the phone to turn on the speaker—without disconnecting the call this time.

Jolene took the phone. "We'll be there." Then she disconnected the call.

Note: I'm writing more history, despite—as has been our practice—not having launched a Dispatch at the end of the last chapter. At this point, we have a lot more history than things to say on Twitter.

So, the brunch.

It was interesting. With the wives there. (Note: all of us carefully avoided calling them the Poop wives.) And pretty much, they ran things.

I was CFTD. In name only. I did get to say, "The meeting will come to order."

Then Jolene said, "The first order of business. We pretty much know what happened with everyone but you, Del, and Oscar. So, tell us."

"You go first," Oscar said.

Del grimaced as if the car in front of him just ran over a dead skunk, and he'd been driving with the windows down.

"Tell them," Eunice said.

Del sucked in a major lungful and huffed it out. He looked at Jolene. "While the other guys took turns watching the front of your house, I watched the back. Your backyard is a nice lawn, but your up-the-hill neighbor's is all trees and waist-high brush. I had on a Ghillie—camouflage—suit and hunkered down in that brush. I had night vision goggles."

"Tell them what *else* you had," Eunice instructed.

"Well. I wore a sidearm in a holster and carried a shotgun and a bullhorn." Del glanced at his wife. "I didn't want to shoot anyone.

"If I didn't have to.

"But I figured firing the shotgun in the air and then hollering over the bullhorn would scare would-be, threat-mongering vandals to crap their pants. Then I figured I could capture the threateners and secure them with zip ties."

"Come on," Jolene said. "What's the rest of it."

"Well, I was watching the rear of your house through my night visions when the backyard floods suddenly came on. Blinded me for a minute, but then I wondered if something was going on in front of your house, so I pulled out my cell and called Hiram, who I knew was on watch then."

"Right," I said. "That's when our up-the-hill neighbor got up to go to the bathroom and noticed the glow from a cell phone illuminating a man's face in his backyard. He thought Del was sneaking up on his house and called 911."

Jolene gave me a look that plain as day said, *You will speak when I tell you to. Otherwise keep your big mouth shut.*

In the silence of my heart, I said, *Yes, Dear.*

"Go on," Jolene said to Del.

"As I said, I called Hiram but got no answer."

"That's because I'd seen Notso come out onto his front porch in his underwear and carrying a shotgun," Hiram said. "I figured he'd seen me parked there, didn't realize it was me, and came to see if I was someone he should be worried about. So, I hopped out and told him who I was—or am.

"Oh. And I didn't take my cell with me. That's why I didn't know Del had called."

"Then," Del said, "I stood there for a couple of minutes trying to decide what to do. Then I heard sirens. Then I noticed the light from my phone, and I figured either you or your neighbor must have seen me and called the police. So, I called Oscar. He'd just been relieved of Circle Duty in front of your house, so, I knew he wouldn't be home yet. I told him to pick me up by the wooded section on Egenthaler Road."

"Right," Oscar said. "We figure I picked up Del about three minutes before the police got there. From what I learned when they were questioning me afterwards, they knew someone had been lurking behind your up-the-hill neighbor's house. From your other neighbor's dogs barking, they figured out how the lurker got away. Notso and Hiram were COPs. They knew there were six of us, so they called Del and me and ordered us to come to the police station."

Del said, "At the police station, they raked us over the coals good. Kept us there the rest of the night.

This morning, they let us go but said we might be charged with trespassing, and maybe a few other things, depending on how the prosecutor sees things come Monday."

Jolene looked around the table. Everyone sat there looking back at her. "All right then. We will break for brunch. While we are eating, we will not so much as mention last night. Meeting adjourned."

I was thinking: *She's trying to be one of the guys* when she snatched the gavel out of my hand and whanged the two-by-four. I jumped as if I had been sneaking up on the back of my house in the dead of night, and Del had fired his shotgun and hollered over his bullhorn. I did not, however, soil my Depends.

Pretty much all of them laughed at the CFTDINO—Chairman For The Day In Name Only. I blushed, and my upper lip grew a sweat mustache.

The procedure at the Post for brunch starts with writing down what you want on a slip of paper. Omelet or over easy, bacon or ham, etc. Then your take your order sheet—and all of us put our own plus our wives on the same order sheet—to the window into the kitchen. We Poops brought silverware, napkins, pitchers of water and OJ, and mugs of coffee to the table. At "Order for—Your Name Goes Here," *you* go to the window and pick up a tray with your food loaded aboard.

When we all had our brunches, Jolene told me to say the before-meal prayer. I did. Then the women started talking to each other. It was as if they were all talking at once, and they thought everyone else's ears were starving for words. We Poops hovered over our plates and shoveled in bacon, eggs, and toast. As if us eating fast would hurry the women along. We had our plates cleaned off, whereas they had nibbled only teensy corners off their platefuls.

No power under heaven was going to hurry them up. They did eventually finish their meals—about when I reminded myself for the one-hundred-eleventh time: *Patience is a virtue.*

Jolene tapped the two-by-four. "The meeting will come to order." Her eyes stepped on each set of eyeballs around the table. Then she said, "We Poop Ladies—"

She said Poop!

"—formed a book club. We read the books on your required reading list. And I read the History of COP Corner through #10. We just finished *The Age of Acrimony.* Eunice," Jolene radiated her I'm-a-pleased-mom smile, "tell them what you said at book club after reading that book."

She cleared her throat. "Early in the book, the author cited how partisan politics was put aside at the beginning of the twentieth century. He wrote that period of cooperation was an aberration."

As Eunice spoke, my mind jumped back to when I read the page she was citing. A period of cooperation in our government was an aberration? Reading that gobsmacked me. As I remembered things about growing up after WWII, the way things worked seemed extraordinarily normal to me. And surely weren't an aberration.

"Give 'em the kicker," Jolene said.

That snapped me back to the present.

Eunice dipped her head demurely. "During World War II and all the way to the Vietnam War, that spirit of cooperation persisted. We should not look at that period as an aberration. We should look at it as a period of what is possible."

"Right," Jolene said. "We agreed that what you COPs are trying to do is commendable."

From the head of the table, I could see five jaws hanging open. I closed mine.

She continued, "We Poop Ladies are in agreement. Even if Del and Oscar get charged and go to jail, you should fight their indictments. And we do not want you to quit the Dispatches. Do you men agree?"

My mouth dropped open. Again.

Hiram stuck up his hand.

Madame Chairperson nodded.

"We haven't had a chance to talk about it yet."

A look washed over Jolene's face. Her annoyed look. I was familiar with it.

"This part of the COP meeting is adjourned." She raised the gavel. I readied myself. She whanged. This time, I did not jump.

She rose. "A glass of wine in the dining room, Poop Ladies?"

Jolene drinking wine! Knock me over with a feather!

The women filed out and closed the door.

"It's getting complicated," Oscar said. "We used to be The Poops. Now we have to say 'Poop Men' or 'Poop Ladies' to know who we are talking about."

"About whom are we talking," I edited.

"One thing's the same," said Norb. "Notso still talks dictionary."

The door to the meeting room opened. Jolene stood there a moment, glowering. "If anyone of you ever calls anyone of us a Poop Lady, ever again, I will personally ram my hand down your throat, rip your heart out, and squeeze it bone dry in front of your face before your eyes go dim."

The door closed.

We sat there.

With our mouths hanging open.

Again.

Oscar said, "I'm not confused anymore."

"You mean about whom we are talking?" Ollie said.

"Yeah. That."

I banged the gavel. "The next part of this Poop Meeting will come to order."

We rapidly agreed to the two points raised by the … Chairperson for Part of the Day. We further agreed that we would send out Dispatch #10 the following morning if at all possible.

Ted Tapman entered carrying a tray with a pitcher of beer and six beer glasses plus a water glass filled with ice cubes and a slice of lime and a can of club soda. He placed the tray on the table and looked at me as if asking if I knew what he was doing.

I knew. "Ted, thanks. But just because Jolene had a glass of wine does not make it okay for me to have a beer. I figure God gave me a barrel of booze to get through life on. And at this point, I've consumed it all. If I'd known I would live this long, I'd have paced that barrel out to last longer."

"Me," Ollie said. "I'd have prayed to the Almighty Bartender for a refill."

◆◆◆◆◆◆◆

Immediately after lunch, I drafted up Dispatch #10. I emailed my draft to the others, and we critiqued and polished it over zoom. That was done by six p.m. I posted a link to the Dispatch on Twitter. I kissed Jolene good night. I went to bed. I slept for eleven hours. I hadn't slept for eleven hours since I was in high school. Of course, back then, I didn't get up every two hours. Back then, we still had an outhouse. Especially in the wintertime, there was plenty of motivation to train your body to just hold it. The way it works, though, as soon as you install an in-house, your body flushes all that discipline and training down the drain. Your body seems to say: *Hey. We have an in-house now. It's no big deal to get up to go five times.*

After we released Dispatch Number Nine, we received a number of threats. Most of them were directed at Gregory Normal, the drafter of these Dispatches. Without informing Greg, the rest of the COPs decided to protect the Normal family. They watched the front and back of the Normal home.

In the very early hours of the morning, the Normal's up-the-hill-neighbor got up to use the bathroom. He glanced out of a window and saw a light in his back yard. Looking closely, he determined it was a cell phone, and it illuminated a man's face. The neighbor thought that man was sneaking up on his house and called 911.

At about the same time, Greg Normal arose for his own trip to the facility. Out a front window, he spotted a pickup parked across the circle from his house. He thought it was one of the guys who threatened him. He hustled downstairs to get his shotgun, loaded it, and rushed back upstairs. The pickup was still there. He decided to find out who was in the pickup.

The guy in the pickup was a COP, and when

he saw Greg step onto his front porch, carrying a shotgun, and in his skivvy drawers, Pickup-man got out of his ride and identified himself.

Just then, Greg heard sirens approaching, and shortly, a line of six police cars, with sirens blaring and lights flashing raced into the Normal's subdivision.

In the meantime, backyard-sentry COP also heard the sirens and figured he might have caused the ruckus. He hot-footed it away and escaped immediate apprehension.

Two of the policemen questioned Greg Normal, his wife Jolene, and Pickup-man, who, it turns out, was Hiram Mudd. One of the police officers recognized Hiram as the guy who'd tumbled reaching for his newspaper the morning after the COP's posted a Dispatch about balance.

Before the sun came up, all of us COPs were taken to the police station for questioning. It remains to be seen whether any of us will be charged with a crime.

Regardless of what happens there, we COPs agree that what we should have done was involve the police straight away, not try to take the law into our own hands. And cause a major fiasco. The Normal neighborhood was not so normal that Saturday night.

Although, one good thing came from that night. The next day we had lunch with our wives at the American Legion Post. After we ate, our wives informed us they had formed the COP's Wives Book Club. They read all the books on our required reading list. One of them had just finished *The Age of Acrimony*.

She said, "Early in the book, the author wrote that the normal state of affairs in American politics was acrimonious debate. But, at the beginning of the twentieth century, a spirit of cooperation and restrained behavior across political party lines began. The author considered that *age of harmony* to be an aberration."

Madame Book-clubber then said, "We should not look at that *age of harmony* as an aberration. Rather we should look at it as an example of what is possible."

We COPs wholeheartedly endorsed this point of view. In *The Age of Acrimony*, and another book, *To Rescue the Republic*, it is evident that the nation was in dire danger of coming apart at the seams any number of times, until it finally did in the Civil War.

We confess to you, Dispatch Readers, our faulty thinking that led to, what we COPs refer to, as the Night of Ghillie Suit, Skivvy Drawers, and Exclamation Points. What we are after in these Dispatches is to get as close to The Truth as it is possible for us to get. The Truth demands that we report on misguided thinking as well the other kind.

We are more determined than ever to continue Dispatches.

On Monday, both Facebook and Twitter blew up with ridicule over our self-protection scheme. At 0830 (zero-eight-thirty), the phone rang. Up The Hill Neighbor (UTHN) Hector invited me and the other COPs to a meeting at the VFW—Veterans of Foreign Wars. The American Legion Post was closed on Monday. The VFW was not.

At 1000, we COPs assembled around a folding VFW table, just like the one at the Legion Post. We sat on folding chairs just like the ones there, too. What was different was, instead of a tack hammer and a hunk of raw two-by-four, the VFW-ers had a wooden gavel, all stained and varnished, and the gavel rapped on a piece of stained and varnished wood, the edges of which had been grooved with a router.

UTHN Hector sat at one end of the table. Farther-up-the-hill-UTHN Arnold sat at the other end. Three Poops occupied each side. A ninth chair. Empty now, had been placed next to Arnold.

Del, to Hector's right, pointed at the VFW gavel and bang-wood and said, "May I?"

Hector nodded.

Del picked up the bang-wood, ran a finger along the router-ed groove, "Hmmm"-ed, and returned the two-by to the table.

Hector tapped the two-by. Gently. Unlike how we Legion CFTDs whanged our crude wood. "We will come to order." Said calm and subdued a bit. Not like we almost shouted it.

Like the VF-ers were civilized while we Legionnaires were crude and primitive. That thought made me squirm a bit.

Hector said, "Arnold is normally up by 0500. He makes a pot of coffee, then he checks email. This morning he found the World Wide Web full of tweets and posts about your confession. Tell them, Arnold."

"Hector's an early riser also. I texted him at 0515, and he texted back right away. We fired more texts to our VFW buddies. Then I, I'm Master-at-arms, convened an emergency Zoom session at 0745. Half the membership was on the Zoom."

Arnold nodded to Hector.

"Arnold said he was outraged at how this whole thing developed on Facebook. The COPs were booted off for expressing their views, while every vile, vicious bit of ridicule heaped on the COPs from the woke crowd was accepted. Like the COPs, all career military veterans, with a combined one-hundred-twenty years of military service—"

A COP hand shot up.

"The chair recognizes Hiram."

"Mr. Chairman, all us COPs are career veterans, but Notso served a total of thirty-six years. Oscar and Ollie twenty-six each. Del had twenty-four years."

I pictured abacus beads moving in the Chairman's mind. His face brightened, extinguishing the frown of concentration. "A total of thirty-two above normal careers. Combined military service of one-hundred-fifty-two years." He beamed like his math teacher had just given *him* an apple.

Arnold's hand shot up. The chair recognized him.

"So, Facebook thought the woke crowd could say whatever The Sam Hill they wanted to say, but the COPs, with a combined military service of one-hundred-fifty-two years had no right to speak their mind?! And they booted you off their site?"

Arnold nodded to the Chair.

For the first time in our lives, we COPs had more to talk about than our wives would have. But, being in the civilized VFW, we spoke in an orderly fashion, with permission, and restrainedly. Halfway close to sort of civilized.

We COPs were gobsmacked. Our own Legion was ready to *boot* us, but the VF-ers told us they *supported us.*

There was a knock on the meeting room door.

"Enter," Hector said.

Ted and Fred Tapman came in carrying pitchers of beer and a tray of glasses. And a fizzy water. Fred was bartender for the VF-ers. He placed two pitchers of beer on the table and departed. Ted placed his tray of glasses on the table and handed my drink to me. Then he occupied the vacant chair.

"Ted. Report," Hector said.

"My twin bro Fred called me early this morning. He told me the VFW guys were all riled up and supported what you were doing."

My hand stuck itself up.

"Notso," Hector said.

"Supported what *we* were doing. You're a member in very good standing."

Ted cocked his head to the side and smiled. Sort of bashful like. Sort of proud.

Hector jumped in. "On the Zoom this morning, we resolved to mount an email campaign to Facebook to reinstate you COPs. We are also emailing the mayor, the county executive, the chief of police, and the sheriff to *not* charge Del or Oscar."

Ted raised his hand.

The Chair nodded.

"When Fred told me what the VFW guys planned to do to support the COPs, I called one of the guys on our post executive council and told him we should be ashamed. The VFW supported the COPs, while the COPs own organization wanted to boot them.

"The council removed Owl Ohlschlager as interim post commander, and they appointed me as PCP."

"That means Post Commander, Permanent," supplied Ollie helpfully. "Not Political Correctness Police."

"It doesn't mean the drug either," from Norb eagerly.

The Chair winced as if he'd just discovered we Legionnaires had become his newest migraine trigger. He snatched up the gavel, then paused. The effort he exerted to control his emotions visible on his face and in his posture. Then he tippy tapped the tap-wood.

"We will," he said. "Proceed in. An orderly ..."

As if he had only enough restraint to contain the emotion that desperately wanted to emblazon his speech, for two words at a time.

" ... Fashion."

He smiled. *Pleased with himself,* I thought. Heck, I was proud of him, too.

PCP Ted raised his hand and, with permission, said, "I want to thank you, Hector, and your VFW brothers at this post, for supporting us, not only for Saturday night but for what the COPs are trying to do, and I propose we adjourn this meeting, and that the COPs reconvene at the legion post to work on the next dispatch."

"Adjourned," restrainedly delivered, followed by, *tap.*

We COPs would like to think we have moved beyond the point where we do nothing but give readers of our Dispatches something to laugh at. But, we admitted to ourselves, that probably will not happen. Still, we are making an effort to get back to our purpose for writing these posts in the first place—to write things that bring us closer together.

One of the things we did at our latest meeting was to remind ourselves that the O in our middle name stands for OLD, old. As such, many of us have suffered diminished physical capability. And here, we invite you to snicker all you want at the notion of diminished mental capability as well.

For example, I, Gregory George Normal, have one leg shorter than the other. The condition causes me to lean in the direction of the short leg. For a long time, I resisted using a cane. *It'll make me look crippled.* That's what I thought.

Anyway, I had to stop jogging some seventeen years ago because it caused such fire in my joints. Walking, though, caused no pain. My wife walked, and we did that together. At first, I controlled my pace for her. A couple of years ago, she wound up in front of me each and every time we did our two-and-a-half miles. She wore a Life is Good tee shirt with a happy face emoji on the back. I hated that emoji, grinning at me not being able to keep up.

Number One Kid gave me a set of walking sticks. I tried them and didn't see that they did me any good. One day I tried one stick on my short-leg side, and, *Holy Moley!* The one stick didn't make me as fast as I used to be, but it sure made me faster than I could walk without it.

What was happening was, as I leaned, I was screwing up my *normal* erect walking posture. And it really slowed me down hiking my short right leg forward when all my weight was shifted to that side. The walking stick helped me maintain a more upright posture, and so my speed picked up. Furthermore, using the walking stick also, in my opinion, made me look less like a cripple rather than more like one.

When I look at myself now, I think of myself as biblical David going out to meet Goliath, and I forgot to take my sling. Goliath laughed, grabbed me under the arms and around my hips and pulled me apart just below my belly button. Then he stuck me back together. Only my upper torso was two inches displaced toward my short leg side. The actual result, I presume, of my body trying to seek true vertical even though I am trying to emulate the Leaning Tower of Pisa.

I look at myself, note how wonky I look, and marvel that I still function as well as I do. And as long as I move beyond *a cane will make me look crippled*, I get along pretty darned well. This body of mine turns out to be a pretty remarkable conveyance in which to ride around the world. Although I used to be ashamed of how I looked, I am now proud of how well my body has adapted itself to being wonky.

Which got me thinking about my mind. One of the things I learned about the mental computer was that it has a finite capacity. When I was thirty, I received orders to the Navy Postgraduate School in Monterey, California. When I started the Aeronautical Engineering Program, we had to take the Graduate Record Exam (GRE). I scored high in literary things and medium in science and engineering areas. My undergrad degree was in Electrical Engineering, but I hadn't used my engineering knowledge in a detailed and practical way since I graduated from college. In a broad sense, I used my engineering background to understand the radar and communication equipment my subordinates were required to maintain on my destroyer. Then, after entering the aviation community and deploying to Vietnam, my engineering background served me well as we developed tactics to counter North Vietnamese Surface to Air Missiles and Anti-aircraft Artillery. SAMs and AAA.

Through college, my first ship assignment, flight training, and two carrier deployments, I always had a novel or a history book to hand. I always read a chapter or more of the current book each day. Based on my GRE, it was pretty clear my brain was twice as filled with literary things than science and technology things.

When I graduated, my GRE scores flip-flopped. High in science and technology and medium in literature. During those two years of postgraduate study, there hadn't been much time for reading anything outside of class work. And textbooks, in many cases, are not literature.

I hadn't really thought about it before. That my brain had a finite capacity. When I started cramming in more and more science and technology, some of the literature stored in there must have dribbled out of my ears.

Interesting.

I also recalled flight training. We SNAs (Student Naval Aviators) were told we should learn to compartmentalize. When we manned an airplane, we were to put everything else but flying into side storage compartments in our brain. Flying safely would demand concentration exclusively on our airplane, not letting it fly into anything, not letting it crash on landing, and making it do its job: killing the enemy or training to do so. So, wife, kids, the dog, and your immortal soul all went into storage. Then, at brain-center, there was nothing but flying.

It occurred that we humans are like that. Our brains have adapted to filling the center of our brain with what is currently most important to us.

Sometimes it is dead on. *The house is on fire! Get the heck out of here!*

Other times, it can be dead wrong. *I don't need no stinkin' cane. It'll make me look crippled.* Or three times dead wrong. Like in *The Oxbow Incident.* "They're rustlers! Hang 'em!" *Oopsie!*

One other thing.

A year or two before COVID, my wife and I took a trip down the Danube River. We started in Budapest and spent a couple of days there. exploring Buda and Pescht. There were museums and interesting architecture, and a grand indoor market, but what sticks hardest in my memory is memorials of the Holocaust. At one spot, on the bank of the Danube, there is a number of bronzed shoes attached to a concrete platform, some fifteen feet, maybe, above the river. The story was the Nazis and/or local Nazi sympathizers would tie some twenty Jewish people, their hands bound behind them, together in a row. Then they'd shoot a guy on the end of the line, and he'd fall in the river, and the rope would pull the other nineteen in to drown.

One bullet: twenty Jewish people murdered. Nazi efficiency.

Those shoes on the wall, some of them were little children's.

The memory of those shoes is emblazoned in memory stone. If I forget my own name, I will not forget seeing those shoes. I've probably read a hundred books about World War II. Some of them dealt primarily with the Holocaust. Others could not tell their story without dealing with the subject. I've visited three concentration camps. But no image sparked from the reading, no impression from the visits is branded on my soul as deeply as those shoes.

I recalled another book from our required reading list: The Age of Acrimony. I wondered what it was that urged, or drove us, into armed political camps as normal human behavior, where an age of harmony is considered an aberration?

Those shoes on the wall at Budapest kept reappearing center brain.

I wondered if we learned very early on what utter beasts, we human animals could be to each other? So we banded together to protect ourselves, but not from saber tooth tigers or cave bears, but from other humans who had banded together to rape, pillage, and kill for sport?

We humans have been killing each other since Cain blazed the murder trail.

Maybe we should try to recognize how deeply this survival instinct, the instinct to band together with others who are like us, and to fear those who are different in appearance or opinion, is embedded in our DNA.

Then, maybe, we can start doing that, to which, the third item in our creed is pointing.

I can hear you, Gentle Reader, saying, "Whoa! A Dispatch two days in a row! How can we be so blessed?"

Here's how. When we COPs were finalizing the previous Dispatch, we discussed including the content of this one in that one, but we decided it would be better to stop Number Eleven where we did and let that content settle overnight before hitting you with this one.

So on to this one.

The urge to band together could be for protection or to beat up, rob, and rape weaker, meeker bands, or to politically mass to thwart misguided souls who, for some unexplainable reason, do not see things your righteous way.

The compulsion, on a personal level, to join a band could be from either of those primal instincts. We COPs imagine that, from the earliest bands onward, a leader of some sort was required. Bands need some kind of cohesive force to hold them together, something more than a shared, in-the-moment, common goal. A leader would provide cohesion and deploy members in defensive or offensive rolls to better the chances of securing clan goals.

In the Ox-Bow Incident, the former Confederate general stomped into the leadership position. In Rules, the author describes the role of the head monk in monastic life. After World War I, Hitler bombast-ed his way into Der Fuhrer-dom. In 30 a.d., Jesus created His own chariot of fire and took up the reins.

We COPs decided, from very early on in human development, the drive to congregate could derive from "good" or "bad" sources.

And from very early on, the definition of those two commodities derived no small amount of shading from the leader of a band.

In our last COP meeting, we pictured an antediluvian cave-dwelling family. Moog was the dad. Mooga his wife. Moogus their ten-year-old son, and Moogina their eight-year-old daughter.

One day Moogina found a baby robin on the ground under the kumquat tree just outside their cave. She said, "Daddy, put the baby bird back in the nest. Please? Pretty please with sugar on top?"

Moogus said, "Poop on that! There's two more birds in the nest. Have Mom make a birdie walking taco for me."

Moog's long chin elongated. His head started bobbing.

Mooga said, "You always side with Moogus. Listen to your daughter for once."

Moog bopped Mooga on the bean with his Louisville Slugger cementing his position as family leader. This, we decided, was several million years before Al Gore invented the phrase "Yes, Dear."

The point of all this is that we should be mindful of herd instinct within our particular species of animal. We should be mindful of its strength, its colorations, and that its leader could be Moog, or Saint Benedict, or Hitler, or Jesus. We should be mindful that leaders and causes, even if we view them as shades of gray; mixtures of true black and true white comprise any shade of gray.

In leaders and causes, we should strive to discern for ourselves the "good' and the "bad," and to resist the urge to jump onboard a particular bandwagon until we have done our due and objective diligence.

COPs' CREED

1. The world is going to hell in a handbasket.
2. It is hell-bent-for-election to get there.
3. There IS something we can do about it. Stop shouting and listen. Seek balance.
4. Find one opportunity to forgive an annoying dweeb every day.
5. COPs must complete the COP required reading list.
6. Number Four above does not apply if the dweeb is packing a gun.

7. Self-delusion is an insidious beast. Guard against it.

8. Before you tell others how to act, examine your own behavior. Do not go easy on yourself.

9. The history of politics in America is one of continuous acrimony that threatened to, and once did, tear the country apart. With some measure of harmony in the political process, both sides stand to gain some of what they seek. And both sides will be better served if the union is preserved than if it tears itself apart.

10. Our country never stopped being great. Appreciate that every day.

COPs' Required Reading List

1. *The Oxbow Incident,* by Walter Van Tilburg Clark. Read the book or watch the movie. Doing both is best.

2. *Rules, A Short History of What We Live by,* by Lorraine Daston.

3. *The Age of Acrimony,* by Jon Grinspan.

Note: We encourage readers of our Dispatches to find their own books to read. We further encourage you to forward those titles to us COPs for inclusion on our Recommended Reading List:

1. *To Rescue the Republic*, by Bret Baier with Catherine Whitney.
2. *Frederick Douglass, Prophet of Freedom*, by David W. Blight.
3. *The Rise and Fall of the Third Reich*, by William Shirer.[*]

[*]New.

The day after we launched Dispatch #12, we COPs planned to meet at the Legion Post. I was looking forward to it. Things were back to normal. We were back on track with our normal way of conducting our business. Write a piece of our history and describe how we came up with the content of our next dispatch. Normal, see? Not dealing with Ghillie Suits, Skivvy Drawers, and Exclamation Points!

Then, Jolene said she was coming with me to the Post. And that she'd invited the other wives.

I heard a flushing sound and pictured *Normal* circling the toilet in a clockwise direction—northern hemisphere, you see?

What I said, though, was, "Yes, Dear."

At the meeting, Jolene was our BWB (Bang-Wood Banger). She brought the meeting to order and said, "Eunice, tell the boys."

BWB paused and stared at me. I knew what she was doing. She was waiting for me to challenge the "boys" characterization of us octogenarian, septuagenarian, and sexagenarians. My head, all of its own volition, twitched sideways. Which clearly meant, "No, Ma'am. You ain't gonna git no challenge outta me!"

Though, I will admit, one part of my brain set to hankering, sort of powerfully, to being a sexa-anything again.

Jolene banged the wood. I jumped. "Pay attention, G. G.!"

For the record, BWB said "G. G." not "Gigi."

"Eunice," BWB's voice fairly dripped with motherly patience, "tell the boys what we did at book club."

"Myself, When I read *The Age of Acrimony*, I dogeared and underlined so many things in the preface and first two chapters, I allowed myself to think I learned everything I needed to learn in the beginning of the book."

Jolene said, "We all felt that way and wondered why the author spilled all the good stuff in the first thirty pages when there are two-hundred-seventy pages of text. It was like a fan dancer stepping out onto center stage with her arms outstretched and all her goods on bright lit display right from the start."

"Not the metaphor I would have used," Eunice said.

I looked at the male faces around the table. They got the picture. I did, too. It made me feel like a sexa-something.

Jolene said, "Eunice read the book a second time and recommended to the club that we all reread it."

"When I read the book the second time," Glenda Mudd said, "I found myself dogearing and underlining in the succeeding chapters almost as much as I did in the early part of the book."

Eunice Sanford said, "Using the fan-dancer analogy, it was like the stage manager trotted out the first act with a 'Tada! Here she is, in all her glory.' And we were gobsmacked because we weren't used to a fan dance like that. And it's like we just got up and left the theater before we realized there were subsequent acts. The follow-ons all put on the standard show, and we missed it."

"But," Rhonda Peabody said, "When Eunice brought this to our attention, it was like the stage manager sent an usher after us and got us all back inside for the subsequent acts."

"You Boys," BWB said, "need to read *The Age of Acrimony* a second time."

She banged the wood. I jumped.

"Time for lunch."

She banged the wood again. I jumped again.

After lunch, the women left. Oscar Wexel was CFTD. He called the meeting to order. We discussed one thing. Oscar closed the meeting.

New world record.

Shortest duration COP meeting: fifty-two-point-five seconds.

Regarding *The Age of Acrimony,* one of the things we COPs discovered was—actually, the members of the COPs' Wives Book Club pointed it out to us.

Eunice Sanford said, "The preface and the first two chapters were so loaded with phrases, sentences, paragraphs I wanted to keep, I dogeared and underlined passages on every page. I felt like, *Why did the author structure the book* this way? *He put all the good stuff in front.* So, once I got that notion in my brain, I pretty much skimmed over the rest of the book. Fortunately, I had enough sense to read the book a second time.

"And what did I find the second time through? I found gems warranting dogeared pages and underlined windows into the heart of the American political animal in the late 1800s."

Thanks to Eunice, we COPs got almost as smart as our wives. We all read the book again, too. She was right. We'd done the same thing she had and missed pages and pages of insights into our history ... and understanding of ourselves.

One of the things I, Gregory George Normal,

discovered after reading the book the second time was that I had to go back and reread our Dispatch #3. In it, we accused the Whippersnappers of jumping onto an idea spouted out on the internet, and without thinking, without so much as a "Could this be wrong?" they mindlessly adapt the idea as their own. Then, lemming-ly, they add their own voice to amplify it and join the stampede.

We pretty much blamed "the Internet" as much as we blamed the thought-lemmings.

When I read *The Age of Acrimony* the second time, I discovered the same sort of phenomenon happened with American voters in the late 1800s. They became thought lemmings. Their Pied Piper, of course, was not the Internet. Rather, a handful of charismatic, persuasive, megaphone-mouthed orators traveled around the country and gave speeches which drew huge crowds. These orators polarized the voters into rabid proponents of one political party or the other, and even those who could not vote, into two highly charged crowds shouting at each other. With neither side able to see any single idea from the other side as having any merit whatsoever.

In previous dispatches, we wrote about this strong, human instinct to band together, for survival, for dominance, for company. This instinct to *join*, we decided, can easily overpower logic, especially when an orator-agitator develops the skill to aim his vocalizations at centers of emotion rather than centers of logic.

Next, we reviewed The COP Creed and Number Seven needed revision. In it, we originally wrote about self-delusion. We decided it wasn't so much self-delusion we were criticizing, but the powerful banding or herding together instinct. Like happened in *The Oxbow Incident*. We want to belong to a tribe, and sometimes to an idea. So, we've amended Number Seven to read:

> 7. Self-delusion, the human autopilot, and a powerful instinct to band together are insidious beasts. Guard against them.

I was on my way to the Legion Post and feeling mighty fine. With the launch of Dispatch #13, I, Gregory George Notso Normal, thought we COPs had hit our stride. We had admitted our inadequate reading of *The Age of Acrimony*. The vein of gold in our mine hadn't played out. We dug deeper and discovered additional buckets of nuggets. Then we worked in *The Ox-Bow Incident*.

Yep. #13 had summed up what we COPs are all about rather nicely.

Clever, I thought quite modestly.

But it occurred, with a little more thought, we could have worked in the *Rules* book as well, you know? Included all three books from our required reading list.

Boogers! We'd lost the opportunity to show the value of all three books on the required list. And to show how those three fit together to build a more complete understanding of our political behavior.

It was 1100, or eleven a.m. for civilians. Bright sun-shiny day. The visor in the pickup doing its job.

I was doing mine. Driving. Negotiating the wiggly-windy street, zigging out to go around a parked car with my driving brain cautioning my eyes to be on the lookout for oncoming cars. But there were none.

From where we live on a hill, there are two ways to get to town. Jolene comes to the stop sign, after leaving the circle we live on and turns left. Then she follows that street until she comes to the major, heavily trafficked Live Oak Street leading to town. Where she has to make a left. Me, I avoid left turns onto busy streets, if possible. Safer, you see? So, I come to that stop sign and turn right.

Now, those streets atop the hill and those leading down are a bit narrow. With cars parked on one side, traffic flows nicely in both directions, but if cars are parked on both sides, quarters are a bit cramped.

So, my driving mind is driving, while my COP mind is going over how we should have included all three Required Reading List books in the last Dispatch. The pickup zigs out into street center to go around a parked car as driving mind shifts to hyperattentive watching for oncoming traffic.

I come to another stop sign. I'm on Maple Street. The cross street is Waddell, and normally, I drive another block east to pick up Apple Street to get to Live Oak. See, Live Oak is busy-busy-busy. Waddell is busy-busy. While Apple is only busy, sort of. But the Street Department is repaving the block of Maple between Waddell and Apple. They've been repaving that block, like, forever. The Street Department only hires two-legged snails. So, Waddell it is.

COP mind crawls into a hole. I look both directions. To the left, the street is parked up on both sides. Once I turn, I will have to pass a maintenance van of some sort with a rack of ladders on the roof and a U-Haul truck, both of which occupy substantial chunks of curbside real estate. Check both directions again. All clear.

Whip a left and push it to forty—in a thirty zone. Thinking: *Get through the crowded section of Waddell in a hurry.*

No time for thinking any Old Poop stuff now. It's all driving going on upstairs. Nobody coming from the opposite direction. *Great plan, Notso.*

But as soon as I thunk the thought, a car turns off Live Oak, heading right for me. As I approach the maintenance van, I move over to the right as far as I can go even though I figure the on-coming driver will pull over and wait behind the parked cars on his side until I pass. As soon as I zip by the van with the ladders on top, I check the rearview mirror on the right to see how much clearance I'd had when I passed it. *Six inches to spare,* I think. *Good job, Notso,* I think. *Eyes back to the front.*

Holy crap! Oncoming Driver did not pull over to wait for me to pass him. He's coming. Like a bat out of hell. And he's taking his half of the road and some of mine! I ease my pickup to the right, figuring to use five of the six inches I had to spare passing the maintenance van. The U-Haul! It's going to be close.

Driving brain shouts: *Not over enough!* But I can't move over anymore.

Oncoming Driver flashes past, and there's a *Bang! I hit Oncoming Driver!*

I check the left rearview. Just Past Me Driver is still *zorching* along Waddell. He didn't seem concerned.

Look where the crap you're going. I looked and took the center of the street until I passed the last parked car.

Then I was at Live Oak. Busy, busy, busy. Took a while, but finally, an opening. I took it, and turned right, and immediately glanced toward my rearview on the right side to see if anyone was crowding me from behind.

No rearview!

The mirror is dangling from a couple of electrical wires.

Drive the pickup, so you don't hit anything else, Dipwad!

Driving mind drove.

Other mind: *Did I hit the maintenance van?* No. I cleared that with six inches to spare. The U-haul, then. I must have clipped his mirror with mine. A picture flashed in Other Mind. A sturdy-looking aluminum tube arrangement supported an aluminum framed rearview mirror on the side of the U-Haul. My pickup rearview was plastic. Probably didn't hurt the U-haul at all.

But that BANG! That had been a giant hypodermic of espresso right to the heart!

Didn't hurt the U-Haul soothed Other Mind, and it sat back from the edge of its seat and relaxed. Driving Mind got us into a parking spot at the Legion Post. I de-pickup-ed and checked the busted mirror on the right side.

Judas priest!

The plastic housing around the mirror had totally shattered. Hardly any of it left. The mirror itself was busted into a number of pieces and held together because it had been glued onto a thin metal plate.

Notso good!

Way not good!

Jolene was always on my case about not driving her side, the passenger side, of our car as well as I drove the driver's side. "Too close to the curb!" "Too close to the garbage cans!" The latter while I'm backing out of the garage as she's hunched forward, attentive to the rearview mirror as a cat hovering over a mousehole in a baseboard.

My cellphone rang.

Poop! Jolene.

"Yes, Dear?"

"G. G. The police called. You hit a parked car. They're looking for you."

With Jolene involved, I was going to have one hundred seven years of bad luck.

As soon as I could work in a "Yes, Dear," I disconnected and drove back to Waddell Street.

I parked across from the U-Haul. Its side mirror was busted, the glass lay on the pavement, and the aluminum tube frame was bent. A cop car was parked in front of the driveway behind the U-Haul. A policeman stood in the driveway talking to a man and a woman.

I crossed the street, after looking both ways, though I'd considered not looking. Maybe that hotrod kid would come back and run me over and help me spend all that bad luck in one fell swoop. But I looked. No hotrod, nor other traffic.

Three sets of eyeballs gored me as I slithered between the cop car and the U-Haul.

The cop's eyes were set about six feet above the driveway. I peered up at them. His sky-blue eyes might have appeared soft if they hadn't occupied such a hard face. That face might have belonged to a Roman emperor in the Coliseum. I looked at the man and the woman. They weren't wearing togi—I don't know. What's the plural of toga? It was a long time since high school Latin.

Anyway, they appeared to have just given the emperor resounding thumbs-downs.

Back to the emp—cop. "I'm Gregory Normal, Officer. I hit the mirror on the U-Haul with the mirror on my pickup." I handed him my driver's license, registration, and proof of insurance. "As I drove by here, I met a car coming the other way. It was coming fast. I thought it was going to hit me, so I moved over as far as I thought I could."

The policeman looked at my proof of insurance card. "USAA. You a vet?"

"Yes, Sir. Navy."

"How long you serve?"

"Thirty-six years."

"Wait just a flea-flickin' minute!" Man In The Driveway said. "You ain't lettin' him git away with this! If my wife hadn't gotten his license plate number—"

"Nobody's getting away with anything," I said. "I hit a parked vehicle. Give me your rental agreement. I'll call U-Haul right now and tell them what happened, and I'll give them my insurance info."

Man In The Driveway frowned as if he'd worked up a good mad and now had no target to fire it at.

"Get him the rental agreement," Mr. Policeman said; then, he crossed the street, after looking both ways, and checked out the remnants of my mangled side mirror.

The rental agreement listed the leasee as Syl Gosling.

As Mr. Policeman recrossed the street, I disconnected my phone call with the local U-Haul office.

"Officer," I said, "I just spoke with the local … guy manning the desk for U-Haul. He did not want to be responsible for making a deal with me to handle the damage to the company's truck."

"You offered to pay for the damage yourself, to keep insurance companies out of it?" Mr. Policeman said.

"Yes, Sir."

"But the agent did not want to do it that way?"

"That's right, Sir."

Mr. Policeman looked at my insurance card, then handed it back to me.

"There's a 1-800 number on here. You should call them."

I called the number from the card and told the nice young women on the other end what happened, that I would send pictures, that I would cover the cost of repairing my own vehicle. I made sure she had my cell phone number and disconnected.

"That was fast," Mr. Policeman noted.

"I've had my vehicles insured by this company for fifty-five years," I said. "In that time, I've made one claim. My pickup truck was in an airport parking lot while I was on a business trip. A hailstorm hit the area. My truck wound up as pockmarked as Pimples Peabody's face. He was a grade school classmate. The insurance company was easy to deal with then, too."

"Pimples Peabody?! Who the hell—"

Mr. Policeman cut off Goose Guy and said to me, "I know your company caters to military people. I wonder if they do business with cops ... Wait a minute! You're one of *them*! A Curmudgeonly Old Poop!"

Mr. Policeman's face bloomed a summer sunshine warm smile. "We were up at your place just a week ago. Middle of the night. Guy in a Ghillie suit."

"What in Sam Hill is going on here?" Syl Gosling

stood arms akimbo. "Aren't you going to write him a ticket? He hit a parked … truck!"

"I'm not writing a ticket. I think Mr. Normal has done what needs doing to set things right."

Syl Gosling pointed. "He committed a hit and run."

"He committed," Mr. Policeman smiled, "a hit, a drive away, a return to the scene, and a fix of the situation. And what have you done?"

"Me?!" Syl said. "I'm the victim here."

"Did you park this U-haul?" Mr. Policeman said.

"Well. Yeah. What difference does that make?"

"You stopped with the tires six inches from the curb. If you had appreciated how narrow the street is with cars lining both sides and parked against the curb, this mishap would have been a no hap. Understand?"

"That's right. Blame the victim."

"Mr. Goose—"

"Gosling!"

"Baby Goose, then."

Syl leaned back as if he'd been slapped. "The mayor will hear about this!"

Mr. Policeman pulled out his cell. Punched in a code. Scrolled. Punched the screen once, twice.

"Mayor Falcon's office," came over the speaker.

Baby Goose spun around and stomped toward the house.

Mr. Policeman said at the phone, "Sorry, Gloria. I butt-dialed you. Sorry."

Goose man's wife rolled her eyes and headed for the back of the van. She grabbed a box from the top of a stack and was about to lift it inside.

"Let me get that for you, Ma'am," I said.

She looked at me. "You're a cripple."

"Actually, Ma'am," Mr. Policeman said. "He's an Old Poop."

♦

It felt as if I'd been trying, like, forever to get to the American Legion Post. Like I'd been driving through rain, sleet, the dark of night. Being struck by lightning, being almost swept away by flash floods, being picked up, me and the pickup, by a tornado and dumped in Kansas.

When I parked in my usual spot at the Post, I felt like shouting, "Kunta Kinte, I found you!" or, "Dr. Livingston, I presume?!"

Those thoughts dosey-doed around in my head. For a moment.

Notso, myself told me, be notso dramatic.

Self, I told myself, you gotta admit, this hasn't been your average drive to the Post.

Then the voice of Jolene told me to "Get a grip!"

"Yes, Dear," I mumbled.

Then it hit me. I needed to call her.

"Are you in jail?! Is this your phone call?! Oh! My! God! Tell me what I should do. Who should I call?"

Whom. She should have said, *Whom* should I call?

"Lawyer," she said. "I'll call our lawyer."

"Jolene! Jolene! Get a grip."

Jolene and I have been going steady for sixty-three years and married for fifty-eight. In those both kinds of years, I never got to say, "Get a grip," to her. She said it plenty of times to me.

"Get a grip," I said again. "I am not in jail. The policeman didn't even write me a ticket. He didn't even write a report on the incident. I called the U-Haul place and our insurance. Everything is worked out. All I did was ding—Actually, I obliterated the crap out of them, but I was trying to help Jolene get a grip—two side mirrors. It wasn't that big a deal."

It took more talking. Jolene wanted me to come home, but I told her I was going to go to my COP meeting.

She said, "When the police called, it reminded me of May 27, 1972."

At the time, we lived on base at Naval Air Station Lemoore, California. I was deployed on my carrier to Vietnam. During Nam, when a pilot was shot down, an official US Navy car, with an officer and a chaplain inside, entered family housing and proceeded to the quarters to inform the spouse/widow her husband had been killed, captured, or was missing.

The wives on base had developed a hyper-sensitive intelligence network. As soon as that official car entered the family housing area, a wife would spot it and trigger notification phone trees. Before that official car arrived at its target destination, every wife on the base knew something bad had happened to someone, and every wife had an ice cube shoved into her heart along with the thought: "(Husband's name goes here) is dead!"

That '72 May day, I had launched from my carrier as part of a strike against North Vietnam. Just after the catapult shot, my engine failed, and I ejected. A helo pulled me out of the Tonkin Gulf. No big deal.

But, when the navy car pulled into our driveway, Jolene thought the worst. To her, for several minutes, I was dead.

In the right here and right now, it gripped my gizzard something fierce when she brought up May 27, 1972. God only knows how many times over my thirty-six years in the navy I'd caused her to worry like that. But I really needed to get to the COP meeting. I had ideas for the next dozen Dispatches, and I wanted the guys to think about them.

"Jolene," I said, "I'm sorry to worry you yet again, but I won't be long. I need to say a few things to the guys. Then I'll come home. Everything really is okay."

I de-pickup-ed and went inside.

In the meeting room, five Poops and Owl Ohlenschlager waited for me. Their eyes were like ten-gauge double-barrel shotguns aimed at me.

Owl said, "You stepped in it good this time, Notso!" His face bloomed a Chucky Doll grin. "I'm calling a special meeting. I'm going to tell everyone you hit a parked car and fled the scene of the accident.

That's conduct unbecoming of a Legionnaire. We'll vote to boot you out."

Ted Tapman entered. "Sit down, Notso." He placed a stupid fizzy water in front of me. "Let's hear your side."

Owl slapped the table. "He'll just spin some load of crap. I got the straight skinny from my cousin, Ralph."

Ted slapped the table. To Owl: "Your cousin is a county cop, right?" To me: "But you dealt with the city police, right, Notso?"

I sat, and all those double-barrel eyes followed me. I felt like lashing out, but our COP Creed pushed its way into my head. Number Three: Find one opportunity to forgive an annoying dweeb every day.

Owl is certainly annoying, and nobody is more dweeby. I forced a teensy smile onto my reluctant face. What raged inside me and wanted doing was to kick his fat butt through the Legion Post and outside and across the parking lot and into the street. Instead, I said, "I forgive you, Owl."

"You … you … you," Owl sputtered spit across the table. Some of it moistened my cheeks. I iron-gripped my hold on forgiveness.

I picked up my fizzy, looked up at Ted Tapman, raised my glass to him, and said, "Here's lookin' at you, Kid," and sipped, and said, "Ahhh."

A smile, as tiny as my own cracked Ted's worried face. Then he rolled his eyes. Then I told them what had happened.

"If you hadn't moved over as far as you did, that other car would have hit you?" Del said.

"The cop didn't even write up a report of the incident?" Ted said.

"Everything blew up so fast because that woman loading her stuff into a U-Haul got your license number and called the police and reported a hit and run accident?" Hiram said.

"But when the cop arrived at the scene, he saw it was just two busted up sidemirrors, not a big deal," Oscar said.

"Except that by that time, the cops had already issued an APB for Notso's pickup."

Ollie said, "One of the policemen who was up at your house the night of the Ghillie Suit called me and told me they were looking for you because of a hit and run accident. I called the others. We were ready to pull the plug on COP Corner because we thought this was another incident which made us look ludicrous. Sorry, Notso. We should have gotten your side of story before gathering all in a lather. Forgive me, forgive us?"

I nodded to Ollie and swiveled my gaze to Owl. I tried to make sure a little friendliness was smeared over my face. "Owl, maybe you'd like to go to our Twitter page. Read the books on our required list. Read our Creed. Maybe you'd like to apply for a COP Membership Card. Maybe you'd like to leave now."

Owl shook his head as if a gnat had flown into his

ear. Then he pushed his chair back, waddled out of the meeting room, and closed the door behind him.

Silence, like soft rain, misted down and filled the room. Sensing that the stillness was mine to break, I let it settle for a moment. Then, "Forgiveness is divine. There is nothing to forgive you guys for, but I forgive you anyway, and thereby, I, Gregory George Normal, sidle up to divinity though I am as humanly flawed as—"

"Owl?" Oscar posited.

Ted jumped in with, "A round of laughter for my friends!"

In which we all indulged.

Then Ted went to get beer, and I told the Forgiven about my ideas for topics for the next several Dispatches.

Del said he had an idea for the next one, he told us about it, and said he'd draft it.

Oscar, Mr. All in Favor, did his thing.

We were all in favor.

So, I finished my fizzy and drove home.

As soon as I walked in the door, Jolene came to me and hugged me, and I hugged her back. We stayed that pressed-together way for a while. Then I told her Owl had spit on me, and I was going to take a shower, and since I'd just been hugging on her, maybe she should take one, too, and wouldn't it be nice if we—

Which is when her port side eyebrow levitated all independent of its starboard mate up nearly to her hairline and stopped that notion dead in its tracks.

I sighed.

As I walked toward the bathroom, I tried to levitate my port side eyebrow independent of its starboard mate, but all I managed to do was wrinkle my nose some and set my glasses askew.

This Dispatch was written by Del Sanford, not Gregory George Notso Normal, as has been the practice till now. Here's why.

Yesterday, Greg Notso was driving to the American Legion Post for a COP meeting. He was driving down a narrow street with cars parked on both sides. A car raced toward him and took up more than its share of the road. Greg thought the approaching car was going to hit him, so he eased his pickup as far right as he could. The oncoming car did not run into him, but the right rearview mirror on the Greg's pickup clipped the mirror on the side of a U-Haul truck.

At first Notso thought he and the oncoming car had sideswiped each other, but that other car kept racing down the street as if nothing had happened. Notso didn't realize he'd damaged his mirror right away. When he did, he remembered seeing the side mirror on the U-Haul being of a sturdy-looking aluminum construction while his pickup's side mirror was plastic. He figured he probably hadn't hurt the U-Haul.

It turned out a woman who was loading moving boxes into the U-Haul, noted Notso's license number and called the police to report a hit-and-run accident. The police called Gregory Normal's home and told Mrs. Normal what had happened and that her husband needed to turn himself in. Mrs. Notso called him on his cell. He'd just arrived at the Legion Post and inspected his busted mirror. He got back in his pickup and returned to "the scene of the crime."

In the meantime, the police issued an All Points Bulletin concerning Notso's pickup. The APB alerted the county police as well sheriff's department deputies. These police officers recognized Notso's name from the incident reported in our Dispatch #10. Word spread around town like a prairie fire driven by a forty-mile-an-hour wind.

At the Legion Post, the rest of us COPs heard the news that Notso had hit a parked vehicle and fled the scene. To a man, the other five of us COPs condemned Notso as a stupid old man who should probably have his driver's license taken away from him. Further, we concluded we did not want someone like him drafting our Dispatches. Further still, we questioned whether we should discontinue the Dispatches all together because we figured Notso had so damaged our credibility people would only laugh at what we posted.

When Notso showed up at the Legion Post, he told us his side of the story. It turns out that Notso spoke with a police officer who had responded to

Moving Lady's 911 call. Notso also spoke with a U-Haul agent and his insurance company. Notso righted the situation, and the policeman did not write a ticket on him, or even write up a report of the incident.

By his actions, Notso had avoided a more serious accident, and he took positive steps to redress the damage.

We COPs should have been proud of our fellow Old Poop, but we condemned him. Just as the people condemned and hung innocent men in *The Ox Bow Incident*.

We learned a lesson.

Gregory George Notso Normal will draft Dispatch #15 and all subsequent ones as well.

The following Tuesday, Oscar was CFTD (Chairman For The Day). Del had finished his project of making us an attractive piece of wood for the equally attractive gavel to tap on. CFTD tapped and called the meeting to order.

Oscar said, "Mr. Chairman."

CF etc. nodded.

"I propose we officially apologize to Notso for lynching him without first hearing his side just like they did in 'The Ox-Bow Incident.'"

Norb's hand shot skyward.

C etc. nodded.

"In *The Ox-Bow Incident*, the innocents did get to tell their side, and they got hung anyway. We'd have done the same to Notso."

Up went Ollie's hand.

Nod.

"As to Oscar's motion, allinfavor."

Five "Ayes," rattled the tiles of the false ceiling of the meeting room.

I said, "Wait a min—"

CFTD tap, tap, tap, tap, tapped the varnished, glistening tap wood. It was easy to see he wanted to whang the daylight out of the thing, but he respected Del's work of art. Or maybe, maybe he was being a model of restrained behavior for the rest of us dweebs.

"The motion is carried," our chairman said. Then he frowned at me. "Notso, as COP Historian, make sure the record shows we apologized to you, officially and unanimously."

I raised my hand.

He nodded.

"Mr. Chairman, I did not agree. It's not unanimous."

Tap, tap, tap, tap, tap. Followed by a glower, and, "Unanimous."

At which point Ollie's motion got notso un-unanimously approved, and I nodded.

COPs can say a lot with a nod.

"Notso," our chairman said, "Have you decided on a topic for the next Dispatch?"

Nod.

"Then you got some splainin' to do," Hiram said.

Our chairman frowned with his forehead but smiled with his lower face as he tap, tapped. Then he nodded to me, and I splained the topic of the next Dispatch.

This Dispatch was drafted by Gregory George Ever So Normal and approved by the COPs. Just so the record is clear.

The topic for today is the human autopilot. Like in an airplane, you might ask. Yes. Like that. Sort of.

In a passenger jet, the pilot can set the autopilot to maintain an altitude, heading, and speed freeing him to talk to the copilot about the St. Louis Cardinals versus the Chicago Cubs baseball game coming up, with the eyeballs of both continuing to scan the skies for mountain tops, other planes, UFOs, and ginormous thunderstorms flashing hot, angry lightning.

Some human functions are on autopilot all the time. Like your heartbeat. Some subjects for thought might speed up the rate. Such as an airline pilot contemplating the hot babe in the second row of first class sitting next to her sugar daddy and isn't that such a waste. Or you might get up from your chair in front of your computer, lace up your tennies, and go for a jog. In these examples, when engaged in physical activity, or the contemplation of a certain type of physical activity, your body autopilot will sense a need for more blood directed someplace, or more oxygen, and your heart rate will increase.

But, you don't think, Okay, Heart, listen up. I'm jogging, so, you know, crank it up a notch.

Another example, breathing. Breathing happens without thinking: innnn, ouuuut, inn, ooooout. Autopilot, see? But if you jump into the deep end of the swimming pool, you are advised to take personal control of your breathing, unless, of course, you are Aquaman. This example is the polar opposite of the first one in a plane. While flying, if you want or need the autopilot, turn it on. In the swimming pool, before you jump in, your body autopilot controls your breathing. After you jump in, you turn automatic breathing off.

Unless, of course, the lifeguard is a hot babe and you think half-drowning might get you mouth-to-mouth. And here's a side tidbit on that sort of situation. When S E X occupies a male brain, a sort of propagation of the species autopilot takes over, and logic is elbowed clean out of the brain. It becomes impossible for the male to see that the babe will be turned off by the sight of a guy puking chlorine water out of his mouth and nose and that she will think: Uh, uh. Ain't propagating no species with Mr. Puke-pants. The human gene pool will be better off without his in it.

One more example. When I was a student in the US Navy's flight training program and learning how to fly in formation with another aircraft, I found out that flying formation was not training my brain and body how to fly tucked onto the wing of my flight lead. Rather, it was training my body autopilot how to fly tucked onto the wing of my flight lead.

We did formation flying in a two-seater. Student in front. Instructor in back. The instructor would position the aircraft on the flight lead's plane, locked in there with nary a wiggle or wobble. Locked in, like the planes were welded together with an aluminum beam you couldn't see. Then the instructor would say to the student, "You got it." Which meant he was no longer flying the plane. You were. And implied with a sledgehammer was, "Keep us in the position I so professionally and effortlessly demonstrated."

But what happens the first few—or several if you look at it as an an instructor—times is the student pilot will see that his plane starts to rise out of the ideal position relative to his lead. He will think, *Holy Crap. I'm rising. Put some forward pressure on the stick. Not too much, though!* So, he pushes on the stick. Now the plane is descending, and the student thinks: *Holy crap. We're dropping too fast. Put in back stick. But not too much.* He puts in back stick and the plane stops descending, and it rises again. The problem is the deviations from the normal position get bigger and bigger until the back-seater can't stand it anymore and he takes control. Which is when the student breathes again.

The problem for the student is that it takes a

second for him to recognize a subtle rise, a second for him to think of the proper response. Another second to push forward on the stick. When the total time available for the student is about .75 seconds to recognize the deviation, understand the correct move, and apply it.

Students all had this problem learning to fly formation. But once he got his autopilot senses calibrated and autopilot stick inputs going, he would be the Ace of the Base formation pilot. And if he became an instructor, he would wonder at this new crop of dweebs who couldn't pick it up as naturally as he did.

Humans, by the way, have an autopilot function that directs the memory as to what to retain and what to trash.

By the way #2: At the time I went through jet pilot flight training, exclusive use of the masculine pronoun two paragraphs up would have been historically accurate. Nowadays, though it would have to be written as: But once he/she got his/her autopilot ….

Anyway, all the preceding was just prelude to the main topic: human mental and moral autopilot.

My wife is dear to me. In those minutes when I allow myself to contemplate life without her if some godawful illness or accident took her, I've concluded she is so important to me that if I lost her, I would be unborn off the earth. She IS that important to me. But let me tell you what happened yesterday.

At our house, things get a little frantic as we

close in on Christmas. Along with other things, one of my chores is to write the family Christmas letter. I've been doing it for fifty years. From early on, I've embedded photographs into the letter. In recent years, photos arrive by text or email, or I snap them myself, and they come in different formats, not all of which are compatible with the Christmas letter app I use. Converting them to the proper format, this year, wound up being annoying and time consuming and extra annoying.

So, I was working on the aforementioned letter when she walked in with a piece of paper in her hand. It was a computer-related problem she asked me to solve for her: Copy the text from printing on a green sheet of paper onto plain old white paper. I contemplated just retyping it, but I figured with a little fiddling, I could do it. Which I did. I scanned the greenie into a pdf document, then exported the pdf into a couple of different formats. Lo! A Christmas miracle! One of the other formats worked.

So, when I finished that tasker, I went back to the Christmas letter. Did I mention that the creation of which was especially annoying this year? Well, it was. Annoying. Especially so.

So, she came into the room to complain there were some issues with the layout of the document I copied. Now I had put the document into Word, with which she has some ability, not necessarily all the way to proficiency. So, she complained to me about the layout issues and never mentioned that I'd figured out how to scan the stupid thing while removing the green background. Not one word of thanks for that.

Autopilot kicked in, and my torqued-off meter pegged against the high end of the scale.

I, Gregory George Ever So Normal, went verbally offensive because I was feeling offended and defensive. Me, who loves her more dearly than I love my own life, attacked her.

Poop!

Then, in addition to all the other crap going on, there was the apology to orchestrate. And it was my mental, moral, emotional autopilot kicking in that got me into that mess. Why isn't there an autopilot function for apologies?

One of the points here is that we COPs decided, at the outset, that although the world was going to hell in a handbasket, there was something we could do about it. What we could do was to tell other people how screwed up they were and how they should change their behavior so the world wouldn't be so hell bent for election to get to hell.

The hell of it is, each and every one of us COPs did just what we were telling other people to not do. We had our required reading list. In those books, we thought, was the fount of all wisdom and knowledge the world needed to square itself away. We COPs all read those books. So, what else did we need to know? It was all the rest of you out there in the world who needed to get yourself as educated as we were.

We didn't need you to be impressed with how

smart we'd become. We were more than impressed. We were arrogance and hubris personified.

The other COPs did exactly what the characters in The Ox-Bow Incident did. They lynched me without even giving me a chance to tell my side of the story. And what did I do?

I did something much worse. I got mad at the love of my life and ripped into her good with sword words.

I admit, Gentle Readers—which we all know you ain't—we COPs considered ending Dispatches From COP Corner for the umpteenth time, but we decided all over again that our purpose in these Dispatches is still worth a lot of effort, and perhaps even more effort than we'd first thought. Getting us American citizens to get along with each other better is still a noble endeavor.

And we've admitted to ourselves that we are humans, and that humans have been screwing things up ever since they ate the apple. But that's not a reason to stop trying. Rather it is a reason, it is <u>the</u> reason to continue trying.

We are resolved to do so.

Until next Dispatch, Gentle Reader.

Hiram was CFTD. *Tap, tap.* "The meeting will come to order." *Tap.*

"Allinfav—"

Tap, tap, tap, tap, tap.

"Shut up, Oscar! We don't need that for the meeting to commence. The Chairman can do that all by himself. *Capiche?*"

Del said, "I move we call our CFTD Oscar the Grouch."

"Allinfavor," said Mr. Allinfavor.

"Aye," as one unanimous voice, less, of course, the Grouch For The Day.

GFTD whanged a divot into the top of the tapwood.

Del grimaced as if GF etc. had whanged a divot into Del's forehead. "I'm sorry. I shouldn't have made the stupid recommendation to change Hiram's name to Oscar."

"Right," Oscar said, glowering at Del. "You can't be giving my name away to any Tom, Dick, or Harry."

"Well, I think the saying should be amended to any Tom, Dick, or Hiram," Norb said.

GFTD looked at the gavel in his hand, sucked in a big lungful, huffed it out, rose, and left the meeting room. He closed the door gently.

"Don't go away mad," Ollie said.

"Yeah," from Norb. "Just go away."

Ollie giggled.

"Ollie giggled like a girl!" Oscar said.

Suddenly, the door to the meeting room ripped open. GFTD stood there like some torqued-off Godzilla trying to decide whose head to rip off first when all five of our heads so needed ripping off.

Well, quite frankly, I was, actually, fairly innocent. Mostly.

GFTD took his place at the head of the table. He laid the gavel, the slender handle of which had been broken, next to the tap wood. Then he placed a six-inch chunk of scrap two-by-four on the table, and he whanged it with a claw hammer.

"Now. This dab-burned meeting of the Curmudgeonly Old Poops will come to fribble frapping order" And he punctuated his statement with a *Whang* and a Godzilla glower. "Notso, what are your thoughts on the topic for the next Dispatch?"

Looking around the table, I could see we all felt the same. We'd been behaving like a bunch of first graders who'd just been informed we'd get an extra half hour for morning recess. Ebullience at this unexpected Christmas gift/Easter egg, months from either holiday, carried us away to the point we forgot about Knuckle Whacker, Sister's ruler. But now we remembered, and we throttled the ebullience back down to humble gratitude.

"Yes, Mr. Chairman, but first, if I may?"

Nod.

"We have had a string of … challenges since we formed COP Corner. Jolene would say these challenges are the devil trying to keep us from doing the good work we might do if he'd just let us alone. So, I propose, as soon as the Chairman calls us to order, we begin each meeting with a prayer."

GFTD nodded to Mr. Allinfavor. He did his thing. We "Aye-ed" the crap out of the motion.

Then GFTD said, "Notso, would you do the first BTMP."

My port eyebrow levitated independent of its starboard mate.

GFTD smiled a *You can do it, Notso,* at me.

"Begin The Meeting Prayer?"

The GF etc. nodded.

"Father God in heaven, help us do Your will in all things, but especially in our Poop business, which it's beginning to look like You called us to do."

Mr. Allinfavor also became TFA (The First Amen-er).

Then GFTD held up his hand to me and addressed Del. "Could you take your work-of-art tap wood, and the gavel, which I busted like Moses busted the first Ten Commandments stone tablet, and build a display case we could hang on the wall here in the meeting room? I think we need a reminder, when we walk into this room that we are not tap wooders, we are whang wooders."

Del said he could do that.

Then GF etc. nodded to me.

I told them the topic. There was no discussion. We had a motion to adjourn. We were all in favor, ate lunch, drank beer—and fizzy—and I got home in plenty of time for *Jeopardy.*

Diskussionsthema verboten! "Just don't talk about sex, politics, or religion!" And, of course, now we have Political Correctness Police moderating allowable discussion topics.

We have talked politics in these Dispatches. Politics is pretty much the point in making the effort to write them, to polish them, to publish them.

Sex, now, we do have a few COPs who–CLAIM TO—remember what that's all about. But all of us would rather watch toilet paper ads on TV than discourse on that subject. So, what's left?

A *Jeopardy* contestant buzzes in. "Religion."

The host grimaces from brain constipation pains. Another contestant buzzes in with: "What is religion?"

You can almost see the blockage molecules evaporate as the host smiles. "That's right. Remember, Dahlia, you must phrase the answer as a question in Double Jeopardy."

Religion. That is to be the topic of discussion in this Dispatch. And why did we feel moved to sneak up on the subject rather than just blatantly flop it out there? Did we think starting paragraph three with "Sex" would hook a certain number of readers to stick with us despite our intention to slither off onto a side trail?

Not really. We intended this opening to be indicative of a process regularly used in politics. First, get readers and listeners eating out of your hand. Then approach them from their blind side with your main point.

We are adding another book to our Recommended Reading List. *The President's Club*, by Nancy Gibbs and Michael Duffy. In the early chapters, the authors paint a picture of how Herbert Hoover became loathed and scorned as having single-handedly caused the Great Depression. Democratic politicians got themselves elected by characterizing themselves as not even remotely similar to the despisable Hoover.

The book goes on to recount how President Truman had become concerned with the post-World War II chaos reigning throughout Europe. Infrastructure and economies were in ruin. Millions would starve if something wasn't done. Hoover had become involved with humanitarian projects, and Truman thought Hoover "The Despicable" could help organize the massive relief effort to save Europeans. The two became friends through their collaboration. But, when Truman was up for election, he found it necessary to resurrect Despicable Hoover as a political enemy and castigated his *friend* publicly. Hoover was reported as understanding what Truman was doing, and once the election was won, the two became friends again.

If Truman's opponent won the election, it was feared the penny-pinching Republicans would scuttle the massive humanitarian relief effort for Europe. If such had been the case, what kind of new Hitler would have emerged from the chaos to lead us into another, even more gruesome, world war? Perhaps that was enough for Hoover to forgive his friend Harry for pillorying him in the press. With Hoover as his whipping boy, Truman won the election by a small margin.

Was a greater good served by committing a relatively smaller sin against a friend?

Some of us believe St. Peter answered that question when former haberdasher President Truman showed up before the judgment podium holding his hat in hand.

Also from *The President's Club*, Eisenhower reportedly despised politics and wanted to remain above such distasteful behavior, however, despite loathing Senator McCarthy, Ike found it necessary to cuddle up to the object of his scorn to win votes in the senator's home state.

Through these Dispatches, we have reviewed our human proclivities to ignore rules even when following them would benefit us significantly. In the *President's Club*, we have seen principled men betray their moral sense of right and wrong to win an election.

I once submitted to a six-word-story contest:

"Ugliest word: Politics. Until anarchy is." A contest judge emailed back: "We don't accept stories like yours in our contest." I emailed back, "I saw nothing to that effect in your entry criteria." I received no answer to that email. I judged the judge had considered she'd spent way more time and attention on a dweeb like me than my worthless male-self warranted. I judged my correspondent to be a young adult female engaged in feminist politics. I judged. And confess that I did. And I considered altering my submission to: "Prettiest word: Politics. Anarchy sure ain't." But I dredged up just enough adult supervision of mind and soul to forbear doing so.

We have written about vitriolic politics being the norm in America. We saw it reported in *The Age of Acrimony*. I came across an article in *The Atlantic Daily*, dated 1 December 2022, which wrote on the topic of the politics of Americans who are a "stew of heated exaggeration, suspiciousness, and conspiratorial fantasy."

We COPs concluded that latter description applied to the current far left and far right of American political life. It's as if both sides channeled their survival instinct from preserving the life of the body into preserving intellectual or spiritual ideology. My body needs air to breathe and there is no compromise on that notion. Neither is there room to compromise on the ideology I cling to. Never mind I have no clue as to why I believe my belief is right and yours is just wrong, wrong, wrong.

Before we started writing these dispatches, we COPs never appreciated our human proclivity for hostile and antagonistic behavior. And, of course, we are not the first ones to preach against these all-too-common traits.

Take, for instance, The Beatitudes.

The meek get to have a vegetable garden of their own, and blessed are the peacemakers, the merciful, and the pure in heart.

Love thy neighbor as thyself. For us today, it is closer to get yourself a neighbor, so you have someone to hate, and you don't have to go far to hate him. Though that of course is an exaggeration. Perhaps.

As we discussed this Dispatch, we COPs realized that what we are after is what the religions we all practice have been after for two thousand years.

Duh!

Oh! We are putting *The Bible* on our Recommended Reading List. And there have been adjustments to the Creed page as well.

Until next time, Gentle Reader.

Norb whanged the wood. He nodded. I said the prayer. He whanged the wood. He swept the table occupants with an I-dare-you glare. Then he said, "The meeting will come to order," and re-whanged the wood.

A weighty, solemn, threatening, dark silence filled the meeting room. I, from the foot of the table, and those to my left, all looked at Del's display case with the whanged tap wood and the gavel with the busted handle in it. None of us, I was sure, wanted to be the one to trigger our CFTD's outrage to the point he'd bust the handle of the claw hammer.

Gavel-handle-busting-Hiram raised his hand.

Nod.

"Mr. Chairman, I think we should discuss the responses to our 'religion' Dispatch. But first, we need to make a commitment here and now, that what we are trying to do is serious business. The frivolous nature at the start of our last meeting wasted time and was this close… this close to turning the whole meeting into a totally wasted COP day."

Oscar started, "Allinfav—"

The CFTD cut him off with, "We are all, each and every stinkin, blinkin one of us, in favor," punctuated by a glower much more powerful than any exclamation point could ever hope to be. Then he said, "Go on, Hiram. What do you think about the responses?"

"Mr. Chairman, when we posted about Trump, we got probably eighty percent unfavorables. This time, on the subject of religion, ninety percent of the responses were negative."

Oscar raised his hand.

Nod.

Oscar's forehead was scrunched up in what I thought was a frown, but his muscles didn't have the strength to pull the rest of his face into a grimace of worry. "One said, 'I thought you Old Farts were posting about politics. In America, we believe in separation Church and State.' What do we say about that?"

Del raised his hand.

Nod.

"Another said, 'You want us all to be Turn-the-other-cheek-pacifist wusses?' Is that what we're saying?"

Just then the door to the meeting room flew open and banged against the wall. In the open doorway, Rhonda Peabody stood arms akimbo, eyes flashing a fierce Go-ahead-I-dare-you-to-knock-this-chip-off-my-shoulder glower at her husband Norb.

The CFTD huffed, "Now, see here—"

Rhonda stomped on him with, "Shut up, Norb!"

I thought Rhonda looked like Wonder Woman standing there in her granny clothes because, well, you know, phone booths are impossible to find these days so she couldn't change into her costume. Then I noticed, well, I noticed her chest. Rhonda is more substantial than her skinny husband. There especially. She wore a sweatshirt, and across that portion, the stick-outey portion, of her body was embroidered:

HERmudgeon.

Then Wonder Br–I mean Wonder Woman said, "We're joining the meeting, and we are here to inform you that we have officially established The COP Corner Ladies Auxiliary."

The ladies, led by Rhonda, flooded into the room. Ted and Fred Tapman formed the caboose. They each carried a card table which they unfolded and set up at either end of the regular table. The ladies all carried a folding chair. One woman carried two. She was Sybil, Ted Tapman's wife. Sybil, as well as every other lady, wore a HERmudgeon sweatshirt.

Ted and Fred wore sweatshirts embroidered with "CURmudgeon."

The ladies all shoehorned their way into a place next to their husbands. Jolene and I moved to the side and left the foot of the extended table for Ted and Sybil.

Rhonda, seated next to our skinny CFTD, tapped

the fancy wood block she'd brought in with her and placed next to our whang wood.

"This meeting will return to order." Rhonda tapped. "First order of business. We ladies debated whether to apologize for busting into this meeting, and after significant discussion, in the spirt of the COP Corner Dispatch, #16, we unanimously agreed, we needed to apologize. So, I, FAFTD, First Auxilian For The Day, on behalf of the other HERmudgeons, apologize."

Ted Tapman stuck up his hand.

Synchronized head nods.

"Fred," Ted said, "Two pitchers, two bottles of white wine, and a fizzy water. Please."

Fred left to do what Ted said.

I raised my hand.

Nods.

I held up one finger. "I move we humbly accept this heartfelt, albeit unnecessary, apology." I raised a second finger (Without lowering the first). " Auxilian is not a proper word, but I move that we adopt it as an official HER- and CUR- mudgeon term.

Oscar said, "In order to save time—"

Karen Wexel said, "we will vote on both of Notso's proposals at the same time. In total synchronicity, they invited, "Allinfavor?"

In basso profundo up to soprano, the response: "Aye."

Norb started, "Now then—"

And Rhonda finished, "on to new business."

Norb: "In the next Dispatch, Notso.—"

Rhonda: "do you intend to continue on the religion theme?"

Norb: "It is hanging out there—"

Rhonda: "without a proper ending."

Me: "Mr. and Mrs. Chair-people, it had been my intention to propose that very thing to the COPs as the topic for the next Dispatch."

Norb: "You said *had been*?"

Me: "It seems to me life may be more complicated now."

Rhonda: "Complicated?"

Norb: "How so?"

Me: "Well, since you ladies have formed an auxiliary, does that mean you are part of our decision-making process for our dispatches?"

The men at the table grimaced. Including Norb. Rhonda elbowed him in the ribs.

"It's not more complicated," Jolene said. "It's better."

"Jolene," I said. "You should have asked for permission to speak."

She replied, "The chairs already gave you the floor. Half of what you own, I own."

Norb: "Jolene, when you said 'better,' you meant our combined decision-making process would be better, not more complicated. Right?"

Jolene: "That's exactly what I meant."

While every man I could see frowned, every woman I could see nodded.

I sucked in a lungful and huffed it out. "Mr. and Mrs. Chair-people, a proposal?"

Nod, nod.

"I propose all HERmudgeons make a communal visit to the powder room."

Men looked at other men. Women looked at other women. Men and women looked at each other. Jolene, with her lips pursed, gave me a, Whatin-heck-are-you-up-to look. I gave her one, which, I hoped, conveyed *Trust me.*

Jolene said, "All in favor?"

"Now just one pea-pickin minute," Oscar growled.

"You were Mr. Allinfavor," I pointed out. "It's not clear you still are."

"Aye," Jolene said, and one-by-one, ayes followed, until the last couple of them were coupled.

Jolene got up to leave. The other women trailed after her.

When the door closed again, Norb said, "What kind of mess have you gotten us into this time, Ollie?"

"What?" Ollie said. "I didn't get us into any kind of mess."

Norb said, "You're out of order, Ollie. I was just making a joke."

"Seems to me, Mr. Chairman," Ted Tapman said. "You were out of order. The CFTD should not make jokes like you just did. The chairman's job is to maintain order and discipline. With your joke, such as it was, you threw order and discipline out the window."

I stuck my hand up.

CFTD shook his head no, and said, "You're right, Ted. We've got two tough things to decide. One: How are we going to handle the HERmudgeons? Two: Once we get that settled, how are we going to answer the responses to Dispatch #16?"

Again, I raised my hand.

This time, a nod.

"The HERmudgeons," I said. "Three main options: independent operations, some participation on their part in our majorly-male business, or 100 percent participation in what would become *our-no-gender-distinction* business."

Del raised his hand.

Nod.

"Notso's right about the three options. And the way I see it, independent operations, no way in hell that'll float. I propose we vote that notion off the island."

Mr. Allinfavor did his thing. Bye bye option one.

Back when I tried to get the women out of the room, I thought it was important that all of us Old Poops agree on the degree of HERmudgeon inclusion in our Poop business. Also I thought I'd have to steer the COP discussion to the rightest answer, but, God bless the CURmudgeons. They saw the way clear to, for us, the right solution.

We brought the women back in.

Likewise, in our equal opportunity discussion of our response to the responses of Dispatch #16, we pretty quickly agreed how we'd handle those.

After lunch, when we left the Legion Post, we were a passel of pleased-as-punch Mudgeons. In the Dispatch which follows:

HER1 is	Jolene Normal
HER2	Glenda Mudd
HER3	Karen Wexel
HER4	Rhonda Peabody
HER5	Molly Fenstermacher
HER6	Eunice Sanford
New HER	Sybil Tapman

In case you didn't notice, Gentle Reader, we have changed the title of our Dispatches. So, our first order of business will be to explain how and why that happened.

Earlier this week, we founding COPs were in the Legion Post meeting room, when our wives invited themselves to join us. We had just begun discussing how we should reply to the plethora of negative responses to our inclusion of the topic of religion in Dispatch #16. The ladies wanted to be part of the discussion on how to frame our responses.

Now, our wives had previously formed The COP Corner Ladies Auxiliary. We founding COPs were tickled they'd done so. It made our organization more like the Legion Post to which we belonged. The Post existed so that male Legionnaires could conduct male business there. You know, like drink beer and talk. To other males. But in this enlightened age, our enlightened Post made room for a Ladies Auxiliary also. A place where wives of Legionnaires could conduct business as well. You know, drink white wine and talk. To other women. And if anyone was enlightened in our Legion Post, it was we founding Poops.

But then the COP Auxiliary wanted to become part of conducting our COP business, our *raison d'etre.* Whoa, Nelly! This was way different from showing them what we'd done after we did it.

This new way to do business, our business, in our former way of looking at things, would NEVER happen. But we invited the women to let us men talk about this … idea they'd proposed. The ladies left. We Poops talked. And here's what the kicker was for us.

If we Poops couldn't collaborate on this project of ours together with our spouses, what in God's name were we doing trying to tell other people how to get along with each other? The enlightenment in that realization blew a sock off each of us Poops. We invited the HERmudgeons back in to amaze them with the magnitude of our self-discovery and the magnanimity of our determination to go forward, just as they'd proposed: together. Equal.

After our revelation, the ladies all smiled, politely, prettily, but we men understood they hadn't had their pantyhose blown off. Then they told us one thing they'd talked about while gone from the meeting room.

"We resolved," HER1 reported for her sisters, "to say, 'Yes, Dear,' to you, our spouses, as often as you say it to us."

Well, that blowed the other sock clean off all us CURs.

But you see what happened there. Every time you pick at an issue which divides a people into two argumentative entities, if you take the least effort to look for it, both sides will find a reason to admit to some fault for the disagreement to have formed in the first place.

"What HER1 mentioned," HER2 said, "is right out of COP Creed Item Seven."

HER3 said, "That's right. And if you look at the whole Creed, you'll see that you COPs did a grand job drafting those ten items."

HER4 said, "And included in the individual items is the notion that you have to work hard to live up to what the Creed calls you to do."

HER5 said, "When we left the room, we found we had to work hard before we arrived at what HER1 reported."

"Going forward from here, though," HER6 said, "there are some things we need to talk about and resolve before the next Dispatch is launched."

The first order of business conducted in the first official combined CUR- and HER-mudgeon meeting was the name of our organization. "Take the word 'cur,'" HER6 went on. "The Internet provides a number of definitions."

"But," New HER said, "we chose to go with a Random House Webster (RHW) offering."

After some discussion, we, men and women alike,

decided we did not want to portray ourselves the way RHW did. We decided the "CUR" in our previously acceptable name had to go. Further discussion also called into question "HERmudgeon" and resulted in a decision to likewise jettison the exclusionary, gender-specific pronoun. A number of New Name candidates were offered, considered, and discarded, including declaring ourselves to be self-proclaimed Melungeons.

We thought about Mudgeons. Trolling the Internet, we found a few sites offering implied definitions of mudgeons as just modern-slang shorthand for curmudgeon. But we decided to not (Note: here we decided, henceforth, split infinitives would be a no-no) But we decided not to be bothered by those postings. We are, we decided, "Mudgeons." Specifically, CURmudgeons and HERmudgeons, with the CUR and HER excised.

Well, by the time we adjourned, in plenty of time for Jeopardy, we CURs and HERs wound up pretty darned pleased with each other.

That, Gentle Reader, is how we arrived at our new name.

We intend to continue these new-name Dispatches under the new, expanded, inclusive, and better management structure.

We also decided to defer addressing the responses to our Dispatch, #16 until #18.

Till then, Gentle Reader.

History of (well, poop, since we changed the name of our dispatches, I guess we better change the name of our history also, though, I am inclined to think: *Is nothing sacred*, as if something called "Old Poop," and our former name being indicative of things like mean and nasty and cowardly could, or should, ever be considered SACRED! I mean—I think I'll just start over.)

History of Mudgeon Corner, #— wait! One way of looking at this thing is that this should be: The History of Mudgeon Corner, #1. On the other hand, since we were Poops, maybe we should title each episode of our history #2, you know, in honor of who we used to be—No. I Gregory George Ever So Normal am not going there. Even with Jolene out shopping while I am drafting this— and here's another thing: I used to write the history without no stinkin help from nobody. I am 100 percent sure when she comes back, we'll just have to start this thing all over again. I can hear her singing: *I did it my way!* But then I realized Jolene wouldn't

**do that. She'd sing: *We did it our way!*
Jolene. Heck of a fine woman. Heck
of a fine Mudgeon.**

**Sigh. Starting over here, Boss.
*Uhgin.***

Jolene returned, and we decided several things:
One. Keep my attempts to start this episode of
the History as it is, because it's indicative of the
transformation the organization has gone through;
Two. Let the above stand as a complete segment of the
history: Three. Have the above serve as a tombstone
over what the organization was; Four. Number this
segment of the History #18 as it was born of the
previous episodes. And, five. End with the title.

Greetings, Gentle Readers. The observant among you will have noticed we began this Dispatch without a title. Stick around. We'll explain.

First thing to note, though, is the use of the first-person plural in the first paragraph. In previous Dispatches, first-person singular made some appearances. That occurrence will have no recurrence. To remind, we formerly CUR- and HER- mudgeons had our CUR and our HER excised. Now we work together in an inclusive and better arrangement.

Though we agree, the new arrangement is better than the old one, this agreement in no way makes acceptance of this approach to Mudgeon business automatic or easy. Falling back into our old, gender-divided ways is always there mentally, subcutaneously, urging us back into our antediluvian attitudes. The point being, transformation is not a one-time deal. It is not a decision you make, and then you just move on because everything has been changed, and it will stay that way forever. This sort of transformation requires, demands a daily, even hourly, even minute-by-minute new decision that: Yeah, verily, I have transformed myself, and I mean for it to last forever.

The observant among you noticed that the first-person singular snuck into the very next paragraph after we promised it would not reappear. In this case, we felt the first-person singular told the story better. The point here being that we need to constantly judge our attitudes, our approaches to business, and our decisions; and to be guided by what we see as the best way to proceed. Even if we have to discard a decision, which at the time, seemed to be ultimately right, proper, moral, and the best way to go, thirteen seconds after making the aforementioned decision.

We Mudgeons believe we have transformed ourselves, become more open-minded, less inclined to join the first herd of moral lemmings that stampedes past. We have confessed how hard the work was to get us to the point where we could make such a declaration, and we further confess, we Mudgeons are all practicing Christians. We are Baptist, Catholic, Episcopalian, and Protestant.

And so to religion. When we mentioned this subject in Dispatch, #16, many of you. Gentle Readers, erupted like a volcano with a sore throat hacking out lava-loogies of outrage.

(Note: The language in that last sentence bothered most of the former HER-mudgeons. Gregory George Notso Normal—erstwhile solo drafter of Dispatches but partnered now in this endeavor with his spouse Jolene—, however, convinced the ladies to return to the responses and reread them. They did and then agreed to let the language stand—for this Dispatch, only!)

Now, each issue of Dispatches has received some negative feedback. But, when we mentioned in #16, that things we were looking for in the ways in which we get along with each other, are the same things Christian religions encourage us to do: Love your neighbor as you love yourself; all hell broke loose in the responses. Restraint was thrown to the wind. Vile, vituperative language flooded our inbox. Several called for us to be banned.

So far, we haven't been banned from this particular social media outlet.

But the thing is, nobody argued against the kinds of behavior we were espousing. What the arguments flogged though, was the notion that these behaviors were associated with religion. As if Religion had become the R-word.

Some of the comments: "We're talking politics here, and we keep Church and State separate in our country;" "god is dead;" and, "You Old Poops were just beginning to make sense, but you blew it when you brought god into it."

The separation issue. "If you're not a (Insert the name of YOUR religion here), you're going to jail." Governments, rulers, should not be able to do that, force people to accept a god with the government's, or the ruler's, designer label stitched to his white robe. Religion should be an individual's choice. We Mudgeons agree and endorse that notion.

At the same time, we note that, while separation of church and state is part of the foundation on which our constitution rests, on the back of our currency, the words "In God we trust" appear. To us Mudgeons, this is indicative of the fact that, at times throughout history, governments, or rulers, have insisted that people behave a certain way, which some, or even an individual, believes is morally wrong. In that case, when you take on your government, you might want to have God to trust in.

We Mudgeons believe carrying on this "religion" discussion, justifying our statements further is pointless. To us, the fact remains that the kinds of "love your neighbor" messages we have been espousing are the way to get us to the goal these Dispatches have been aimed at.

So, going forward, we are not retracting anything. We are not apologizing for any points we've made. We will, however, continue to listen, to be attentive to your responses, including your lava-loogies. But after we listen, we will do what our consciences guide us to do.

When we started these Dispatches, we had no intention of making any kind of connection with what we were saying to religion. It just turned out that fifteen Dispatches into our mission, we recognized that some of the things we have been saying have been said for thousands of years. By religious people.

So, we end this Dispatch with: Thank you, God, for this Divine Coincidence.

Till next time, Gentle Reader.

P.S. We put the title at the end because, to us, our transformation resulting from including HERMudgeons into our CURmudgeon business, and then surgically removing the HER- and CUR- from our name, was as radical as turning us upside down. The dictionary we consulted defined curmudgeon as: 1. a mongrel dog, especially a worthless or unfriendly one; 2. a mean, cowardly person. In discussing this, we—men and women alike—agreed we former CUR-s did not fit that description. We male Mudgeons further agreed that as long as we were CURmudgeons, including "Old Poop" in our name was just fine. However, comma, once we included our spouses, our Beloveds, into our group, both of those two words became more inappropriate than "cur" turned out to be.

In the interest of full disclosure, as we discussed transforming our name, one male Mudgeon disclosed that his wife had a needlepoint on the wall of their bedroom which read:

**Lorena Bobbit
You go, Girl**

Which, for him, was all the reason he needed to vote to remove "Old Poop" from the name of our group. The rest of us male Mudgeons, however, supported excluding those two words based on totally rational thinking.

On Monday evening, the Mudgeons held a Zoom meeting to consider inviting Ted and Sybil Tapman to become full-fledged Mudgeons. We also elected a Mudgeon Chaplain to serve a one-year tour of duty. We elected Jolene Normal. The meeting lasted ninety seconds.

Tuesday morning, Co-chair Mudgeons For The Day (CMFTD), Sybil and Ted Tapman called the meeting to order, Sybil tapped the tapwood, and Ted invited Jolene to say the prayer.

Jolene rose from her place at the foot of the table and hung a sign on the wall opposite the meeting room entry door. Already hanging there were two display cases Del Sandford had made. One case held the damaged tap wood and broken gavel. The other contained the whang wood and the claw hammer. These were indicative of who and what we'd been. Jolene's sign indicated what we'd become and what we'd work to hang onto.

Her sign read:

Choose
HUMILITY

Then she read the Beatitudes from her Bible and reminded us that those eight "Blessed ares" called us to a life of humility and love rather than one of aggression and greed.

After, "Amen," Sybil tapped, and Ted said, "Business: new or old?"

Notso raised his hand.

Nods.

"The Chaplain and I discussed her sign idea last night," Notso said. "She plans to do a new sign for each meeting. "Choose" will remain the same, but there will be a new virtue we are invited to take into our hearts for each meeting. The new virtue will be penned onto paper and taped over the previous one. What she plans to do at subsequent meetings is to pray that we remember the day before's virtue, then tape a new one on top of the old, and we will pray to live up to that new one as well."

"Take up the new one without forgetting the previous one," Jolene said, "because the Beatitudes are a set. No one item is complete unto itself."

"Would you like to give us a preview of a coming attraction, Chaplain?" Notso said.

"Yes, Dear," she said and smiled humbly. "Next, I had planned to present "Choose Light" on the sign.

Sunday at church, we sang *We are the Light of the World*. After Mass, Notso and I discussed this and agreed that this is what *our* Dispatches are attempting to do. To serve as a guiding light to our readers. Through our actions, enfolding the things in our Dispatches into our own hearts before we ask others to embrace these things as well. We serve as examples of the kind of behavior we invite others to emulate."

"But," Notso, quite smoothly, added, "we decided before we invited ourselves to accept the notion that we are models of behavior for others 'Go and do likewise, like we did,' we should first dump a boatload of humility into our hearts. Thus, choose HUMILITY." And Notso smiled at his wife, rather proudly.

Hiram raised a hand.

Nods.

"Good stuff, Chaplain."

"And Notso, good on you, also," Glenda Mudd added.

Oscar raised his hand.

Nods.

"What about the Commandments?"

"Shouldn't we put something about them in our Dispatches?" Karen Wexel said.

After Karen's input, Notso noted a Lorena-Bobbit-like look of irritation flit across his wife's face. Then, she closed her eyes, took a deep breath, let it out, opened her eyes, smiled sweetly, and said, "Good idea.

I think we might do a Beatitude in one Dispatch, then a Commandment, then another Beatitude, and so on."

A look of surprise and chagrin flooded Jolene's face. "Sorry, Cochairs. I forgot to ask for the floor."

"Your sin," Sybil tapped.

"Is forgiven," Ted said.

Del raised a hand.

Nods.

Del wanted to talk about Commandments. And the group did discuss the subject. Before it ended, Notso Normal wound up sobbing, with tears streaming down his face and snot running into his mouth.

When we discussed what would go into this Dispatch, we noted again how what we set out to do with these postings mirrored behaviors our Christian religions called us to embrace. To us, it is fact, and not to be avoided because some of you, Gentle Readers, want god to be dead. To worship, we suspect, hedonism instead.

We hasten to apologize for the judgementalism inherent in that last statement, but in the interest of factual reportage, we'd be remiss if we did *not* point out that we Mudgeons have observed a number of younger people behave as if self-centeredness were their religion. We have seen it on the highways when a person attempts to enter a freeway, and drivers in the far-right lane do not slow down to create a space for the wannabe entrant. Rather, those drivers act as if they cannot be bothered to even notice another person is trying to get onto the roadway.

And even going into church, people from the Mudgeon generations typically look behind them to see if someone else is coming, and if such a follower is there, the Mudgeons will hold the door for them. Young people these days do not even turn to see if a cripple, or anyone at all, is behind them.

This last, judgmental, again. We know. But necessary. Again, forgive us. Please. And, thank you.

As to religion, or religious themes, when we consider it necessary, or relevant, we will continue to include such in these Dispatches. Furthermore, we confess, we have made opening our Mudgeon meetings with a prayer a standard practice. A part of this opening prayer is to ask God in heaven to watch over those of you who wish Him to be dead. And at our last meeting, we appointed a chaplain to lead us in our prayers.

At the last meeting, Chaplain Jolene Normal told us how the Beatitudes pointed directly to the kind of behavior the Mudgeons espoused in these Dispatches. Love thy neighbor instead of beating him up—whether physically or figuratively—and taking from him something you covet. The purpose for adopting these types of behaviors, the chaplain went on, is to get to a way where the people, who now are separated by a political Grand Canyon and shouting at each other from rim to rim, can both get some of what is so important to them.

In ensuing discussion, some Mudgeons proposed including treatment of The Commandments in the next, this, Dispatch. Our chaplain proposed that we first deal with The Beatitudes, then take on The Commandments.

A Mudgeon pointed out that The Commandments were bedrock, fundamental, and came first. They were "Thou shalt nots." Much later in history, Jesus gave us the Beatitudes. These were "Blessed are those who do a certain thing." "Different approaches," the Mudgeon pointed out. "One is 'Don't do these things.'" The other is 'Blessed are you if you do these things.'"

Another Mudgeon said, "The Commandments are sacred to us. Don't cuss, kill, lie, steal or even covet."

But all us former CURs were members of the US Armed Forces. As such, we killed, or were prepared to do so. *Ecclesiastes* says there is a time for everything, every affair under the heavens. But, did any of the CURs say, "Oh, all right then, and pull the trigger?" As if there was nothing more to it than picking your nose when no one was looking?

To a man, our CURs all said the killing, the destruction they rained on the enemies of our country, saddled them with a heavy moral burden. Ecclesiastes may have offered *it's okay to kill* in certain circumstances, but there was one thing that section of that book did not offer, which, to a man, the CURs felt they needed. That need was absolution.

One former CUR said, "I struggled at times with notions like: 'I have turned into a cold-blooded killer. I am not fit to be a father to my children.'

"1971. Flying missions from my carrier took over the center of my brain. I had flown one-hundred combat missions over, mostly, South Vietnam and

Laos—the LBJ bombing halt of the North was still in effect—for American fighting men, but it was pure opportunity for the North Viets. The pilots on my carrier called the missions we flew "making toothpicks. We blew up trees searching for trucks the North Viets drove at night but hid in trees during daylight hours."

All the pilots on his carrier and mine were frustrated with the bombing halt. It meant that the enemy had all of their own country to move war supplies to the border of our ally as free from threat as a trucker on an American highway. Furthermore, after three years of bombing halt, there was no interest on the part of the North Viets to negotiate. And that had been the announced purpose of the bombing halt.

Our confessee admitted to thinking he should have said, "Oh, yo! Pentagon, Mr. President, this bombing halt thing. It! Is! Not! Working!" But he said he just swallowed it, said, "Aye, aye, sir," and made more toothpicks.

"Still," he continued, "I got so caught up in flying my missions off my carrier, I forgot about the sailors in my division. One kid, he was seventeen, had a father die. His mother had died two years prior. He got depressed and jumped off the fantail. Nobody saw him, but he left a note."

The man shook his head. "I got so wrapped up in those missions, hoping that one day, I'd get credited with blowing up a truck and killing a couple of gomers, I blew off my responsibilities to the kids the navy put me in charge of."

That Mudgeon's confession smacked into me like I was in a crosswalk with the "walk" sign illuminated when a semi going sixty-five hit me.

That Mudgeon had one failure to prevent a suicide in the sin-closet of his soul. I had two of those. Plus two sailor lives lost that I should have saved. With that realization, I started crying like a baby.

I am sure, Gentle Reader, you do not want to hear my confession of all these sins. With my hearing aids cranked up, I can hear you yawn. But, I figure I owe you one.

Previously, I mentioned the ship I'd been assigned to prior to commanding an aircraft carrier. This was an amphibious assault ship. We could carry two thousand US Marines plus a goodly number of helicopters. One day, in the middle of a large exercise, with a full load of Marines aboard, the flight deck crew found it necessary to employ a rarely used helo takeoff and landing spot. I was on the bridge, and when this extra helo cranked up its engine, I called the Air Boss and asked him about the helo on the extra spot.

"The Flight Schedule says we have to use it, Skipper," he said.

"Boss, that helo is parked right where the Marines come up from below to enter the flight deck."

During actual combat ops, or training, twenty or so Marines were led by a sailor to one of the helos spotted along the port side of the flight deck. Once the sailor delivered the Marines to their conveyance ashore, he returned below decks. My concern was that in all the operations we had done to date, no sailor in our crew had ever led his line of Marines past a helo on that landing spot. Tail rotors were deadly weapons, and the guys coming out from below decks would have to pass close to the tail rotor on that extra spot.

"Boss," I said, "make sure—"

At that point there was an announcement of an emergency on the flight deck.

A young sailor had led his twenty Marines out from below decks. The extra helo had its rotors turning, and the downdraft from the main rotors made him duck his head and he walked right into the tail rotor.

A nineteen-year-old—I always think of him as a kid—Reggie. I see his face once a week. On a Tuesday, when I get his coffee mug out of the cabinet for what I call my *mourning cup of Joe*. Tuesday/Reggie's mug is emblazoned with a decal logo of the ship we crewed together, Reggie and me. And the mourning bit, of course I mourn for the man I killed, but I also mourn for the man I should have been. But that man did not show up for work that day. The man who did show up was five minutes late and a precious life short.

On other days of the week, I have mugs for the two suicides I should have prevented, but did not. I have another mug for the other dead sailor I should have kept alive, but did not.

Another thing I should have done was to confess

those sins. But I did not do that either. They were sins to me, but I did not want to drag them out of my soul sin-closet for anyone else to see, not even my priest.

For decades, I've used my Mourning Mugs of Joe to remember these men, and one woman. And I convinced myself that was good enough.

Through our discussions since forming COP Corner—recently metamorphosed into Mudgeon Corner—and in drafting and polishing our Dispatches, all of which call on you, out there in web land, to change, I have come to see it is me who needs to change more than any other person on the planet.

I share this with you because somewhere, out *there*, is the person second most in need of changing. If my experiences help that person a single smidgeon's worth, then Thank You, God.

This Dispatch was drafted by Del Sanford. Our purpose here is to announce that Gregory George Normal passed away a week ago. He had the ideas for most of the topics covered in previous editions. He drafted the Dispatches as well as a companion history to document the discussions we Mudgeons had before issuing a new post.

Of course, we miss the heck out of Notso, and we haven't decided if we Mudgeons can get along without him. When we do decide, we will let you know, Gentle Reader. That's the way Notso addressed you, and I think he would agree. Maybe this Dispatch has turned you truly into just that.

Anyway, there will be at least one more Dispatch. Till then, GR.

This episode of the History is being written by Jolene Normal.

Two-and-one-half weeks ago today, I discovered my husband, Gregory George Normal, slumped over the laptop at his rolltop desk. GG usually woke between oh four and oh five hundred. His routine is—was to unload the dishwasher, eat breakfast, and sit at his desk and write. I get out of bed at oh seven, and I found him at oh seven fifteen.

He wrote—writes wants desperately to be placed there—everyday. He has self-published one book and has been working on a second one for probably four years now. Plus, he spent a lot of his writing time on Mudgeon business the last several months.

His head rested on the keyboard of his laptop. When I pulled him back, he wasn't breathing. He had no pulse. He was cold.

In a Mudgeon Dispatch, or it may have been in a Curmudgeon one, GG wrote about human autopilots. That's what got me through that day and the next ones. My autopilot turned itself on. And I am not over what happened. I never will be, but I believe I can now turn off the autopilot and steer myself.

Back to that day, after calling 911, I called our oldest daughter and told her. She set up a group Facetime with her sisters, and we told them.

The rest of that day is a blur, but I know I called Eunice Sanford. The Mudgeons needed to know.

It was this morning at oh seven fifteen when I turned my autopilot off. At oh seven sixteen, I called Del and Eunice Sanford.

Eunice picked up. Caller ID must have told her it was me.

"Jolene! How are you? What can we do to help? Do you need anything? Anything at all?"

"I'm coping, and, no, I don't need anything. I wanted to tell you what GG was doing when …." I took a breath and exhaled. "When he passed. He was writing a letter of resignation from the Mudgeons. I'd like to email it to you. Perhaps you and Del can read it. Then call me back. Okay?"

I emailed them a copy of the letter and hung up. Five minutes later they called back. They were on speaker phone.

Del said, "That letter, man. As we went through our Curmudgeon and Mudgeon efforts, I thought I got to know Notso. I thought I could see into the depths of his soul. That resignation letter took me so much deeper. What an incredible experience it has been to have a front row seat on what turns out to have been a journey of self-discovery for Notso."

"No," I said. "It wasn't a journey of self-discovery. It was a journey to discover ways for people to get along with each other better. And you cannot make progress on that journey unless you embark on a side-by-side one of self-discovery."

"That sounded so Notso."

"Notso," Eunice said, "and all of you poops, set out to see if you could find a way to bring people closer together. To do that, you at first told people how they needed to change. But you all, and maybe especially, Notso, started applying your behavior modification suggestions to yourselves, too."

"All of you former CURmudgeons are better men than you were before COP Corner," Jolene said.

"And all of us former HERmudgeons are better women than we were before, too" Eunice said.

"Where are we going with this discussion?" Del said.

"You want to tell him, Jolene? Or should I?"

"You say it."

"We need to keep Mudgeon corner going."

"What? We already decided we were pulling the plug on Mudgeon Corner. I was going to send out the email after our next Wednesday get together."

"You male Mudgeons decided," Jolene said.

"With half the voting membership absent," Eunice added.

"We need a meeting with all the members present," Jolene said.

"We need to discuss Dispatches from Mudgeon Corner," Eunice said.

"Then we need to vote on it," Jolene said.

"If we decide to keep Mudgeon Corner going, who's going to draft the Dispatches and write the history? None of us want to do it. That's why we decided to pull the plug."

"I'll write the history," Jolene said, "and I'll draft the dispatches."

"And," Eunice said, "all us Mudgeons, I say again, *all* of us Mudgeons will give Jolene *all* the help she needs."

Quiet flowed in both directions over the phone lines. Then Jolene said, "Del, if I may be so bold as to suggest a 'Yes, Dear' would fit in here very nicely."

"Jolene, you are Even Less So Normal than Notso was."

"In a sentence like that, I've started using the present tense."

After another short pause, Del said, "Yes, Dears."

At lunch at the American Legion Post, everybody avoided talking about Mudgeon business. To a man, the Mudgeon men were uncomfortable. It almost seemed as if they weren't even interested in eating. Imagine that. Men not interested in eating!

The Mudgeon wimmen—

That thought just popped into my head as such a GG thing to think. Extra moisture formed a tiny bubble on my lower eyelids. I backhanded them away.

However, the Mudgeon wimmen, including me,

ate and talked about quilting, church ladies' sodality, and the Hospital Auxiliary Trivia Night coming up. And of course, kids, grandkids, and great grandkids. Wimmen do that sort of thing better than males. In my opinion.

When we finished eating, Hiram stood up and invited the men to help him clear the table. I was sure he wanted to get the men out of the meeting room to talk about what they would say in the Mudgeon meeting, which would start when they got back.

The door to the meeting room closed behind last man out, and I said, "I'd like to serve as Chairwoman For The Day. Any objections?"

There were none.

I stood up and took the display case with the whang wood in it down from the wall,[1] removed the back of the case, and lifted out the claw hammer and wood.

> Note: This is the first episode of
> Mudgeon History to use a footnote. I
> feel proud in a very humble way.

The women sat at the table with an empty chair beside them. I sat at the head. Eunice sat to my left. She placed a hand atop mine, and I could feel my

---

[1] Ted had said we could keep Del's displays hung on the wall. If for any reason they needed them to come down, they'd be stored in a cabinet in the front of the meeting room.

sudden spike of grief drain out of my heart, down my arm, and into her hand. I smiled her a wet-eyed thank you. She smiled a wet-eyed "I wish I could take all of it from you."

Shuffling feet and mumbling men approached the meeting room door. The door opened. Hiram Mudd took a step forward and stopped. Those behind bunched against his back.

Hiram's eyes locked onto mine. I was sure he felt like he needed to say something.

I beat him to it. "Come in. Take a seat."

Hiram moved into the room, the others in file. He said, "We decided we wouldn't have a formal meeting."

"We decided we would," I said.

"Seven to six," Glenda Mudd said. "Majority rules."

"Uh. I abstained," Del said.

Ted had too.

Hiram stood behind his chair. "We could just walk out."

"You could," Karen Wexel said.

"If I were you," Rhonda Peabody said. "I wouldn't."

Ollie Fenstermacher sat. "I ain't leaving." He looked around the table. "None of us are."

I grabbed the claw hammer and whanged the whang wood a good lick.

The men jumped, and I stared at the tabletop. It seemed as if I wasn't just me anymore. I was me, but I was also GG.

Eunice squeezed my hand.

"The meeting will come to order. First order of business: Do we keep Mudgeon Corner going? Discussion?"

"Jolene," Hiram began, but I cut him off with a whang.

"You want to speak, you raise your hand. You speak after the Chair, in this case, Chairwoman recognizes you." Punctuated with a no-nonsense Chairwoman glower.

He raised his hand.

Nod.

"We're concerned about you, Jo ... Madam Chairwoman. We think you need some time. You know, to adjust. Heal."

"Thanks for your concern. I appreciate it more than I can say. As to healing, I don't expect to heal. Ever. I'm not sure I want to. And I don't want, or need, time. What I do want is to keep the Mudgeons going. I saw what the group you all formed did for GG. I know what it did for me. We all agreed when we cut the CUR and HER from our group names, we became better than we'd been before."

Molly raised her hand.

Nod.

"Better as individuals, better as CURmudgeons and HERmudgeons, and better still when we married the two groups of us into Mudgeons."

"Any other discussion?"

Hands remained tabletop. I nodded to the Wexels.

"All in favor?"

It seemed solemn, with those spaces between the words.

Unanimous, though it took two elbows to ribs to make it turn out that way.

"Second item: Writing the history and drafting the Dispatches. I volunteer to do those. And Sybil Tapman has agreed to take meeting minutes if I serve as Chairwoman. Discussion?"

There was none. The vote: a unanimity of elbow-free "ayes."

"Item three. After GG passed, I found a copy of *Tombstone* by Tom Clavin on his 'to-read pile'. I will tell you I am only fifty pages into it, but I told Karen Wexel about it, and she put it on her Kindle. She read it. Would you give us your book report, please?"

"Happy to, Madame Chairwoman. I had never read a book about that gunfight at the OK Corral before. I have watched … any number of movies about it. From each of those movies, I always got the sense there was closure of a kind. Like the gunfight finally settled a long simmering feud between the good guys and the bad guys. According to this book—she held up a copy—there was no closure for a long time afterward. Wyatt Earp and his brothers were charged with murder. The law in that corner of the frontier was slanted toward ranchers and cowboys, who in actuality, were rustlers and robbers and cold-blooded killers. And my most abiding take-away from the book was the feeling that if law and order as practiced in that part of our country was the norm, then it's a good thing the constitution gives us the right to bear arms. Because around Tombstone, dog eat dog was the law of the land, and the 'good' people could only hope to survive if, somehow, they managed to escape drawing the attention of the bad guys to themselves."

Eunice raised her hand.

Nod.

"I read the book, too. I think we should ask all the Mudgeons to read it. Ten days from now, we should vote as to where the book goes, on the required or the recommended reading list."

"Do you have an opinion as to which list it belongs on?"

"Yes, Madame Chairwoman. It belongs on the required list."

"Get the book. Read it. We'll discuss it. We'll vote as to which list we add it."

I pulled a folder from GG's briefcase. From it I took copies of his letter of resignation and passed them out, one to each couple. "Read this please. In two days, I'd like to have a meeting to discuss the letter and to address it in our next Dispatch. I should have a draft done by then for Board of Directors to review."

"Any other business?"

There wasn't.

We adjourned.

In time for Jeopardy.

That night I set my alarm for 0500, and by 0545, I was at the laptop.

I typed:

Time passed. I looked at the time in the corner of the laptop window. 0551. For six minutes I'd been waiting for my fingers to start typing words. But my fingers were more silent than GG had been during COVID sequestration days.

"Fingers," I mumbled, "I'm laying a hundred-word requirement on you in the next—"

I thought about typing in high school. I'd gotten up to forty-five words a minute. My fingers now, though, would never produce so many error-free words in a minute. I needed a number. I picked one.

"I'm laying a hundred-word requirement on you every ten minutes."

Time passed.

Lord, let this cup pass from me.

I shivered. Over my nightgown I had on a robe and a sweater over that.

Not my will, But Thine be done.

I felt warm, opened my eyes, sat forward, removed the sweater, and placed my hands on the keyboard. They began to type:

I am Jolene Normal, wife of Gregory George, and I have picked up my husband's duties of writing our Mudgeon history and drafting Dispatches. I will begin by telling you about how I found my husband almost three weeks ago now. It was here, where I am sitting, at his laptop atop his rolltop.

I found him slumped over, his forehead resting on the keyboard. He wasn't breathing and he was cold. I called 911.

Previously, GG wrote about the human autopilot. I confess, I didn't really get it when I read what he wrote in the History and in the Dispatch on the subject. But I get it now. My autopilot took over that day right after the 911 call, and I've been letting it drive me around during the weeks since I found him. Two days ago, I felt like I could finally turn it off.

I read over what I'd written and corrected a couple of typos. Then I prepared to start writing again, but I froze.

I felt GG behind me. I turned around. I still felt him behind me.

Jolene. Turn around and write.

I turned.

GG had suffered a stroke. He'd been on a blood thinner for four years. We found out he'd stopped taking them at Thanksgiving. That holiday, this past year was frantic for us. We normally had Thanksgiving dinner for the family at our house, and we were prepared to do so, but our daughters decided they should relieve us of the necessity to do all the work it took. But that didn't get decided until the last minute. Getting ready for such a feast, GG always moves his pill box from the kitchen counter to his man room, because we use the counter to stage the food. This year with all haggling over whether we were too old to handle it or not, and with all the Mudgeon business going on, GG forgot to take his pills.

When I found GG, he had just finished typing his letter of resignation from the Mudgeons. I'm going to include his letter here.

I, Gregory George Notso Normal being, for the first time in a long time, of sound mind, and a body, which left sound in the rearview mirror so long ago it's disappeared, do, hereby, tender my resignation to the Mudgeons.

During the last Board of Directors meeting, one of our members confessed to harboring a sin deep in his soul. When he was on active duty, and a lieutenant, one of the sailors in his division committed suicide. Our confessor was a pilot and flying missions over Vietnam, and he got so caught up in flying his missions, he totally stopped worrying about the young men in his division. It took him fifty years, and the Mudgeon's efforts to bring people together that made him look deep within himself and discover that old sin.

When he made that confession, it hit me hard, because I have two of those failure to prevent suicide sins on my soul, plus two lives I should have saved but didn't.

I am sure, Gentle Reader, you do not want to hear my confession of all these sins. With my hearing aids cranked up, I can hear you yawn. But, I figure I owe you one.

Previously I mentioned the ship I'd been assigned to prior to commanding an aircraft carrier. This was a helicopter carrier amphibious assault ship. We could carry two thousand US Marines plus a goodly number of helicopters. Our flight deck was marked with parking spots and takeoff and landing spots for the helos. One day in the middle of a large exercise with a full load of Marines aboard, the flight deck crew found it necessary to use a rarely used helo takeoff and landing spot. I was on the bridge, and when this extra helo cranked up its engine, I noticed this and called the Air Boss and asked him about the helo on the extra spot.

"It's a big exercise, Skipper," he said. "We need the spot."

"Boss that helo is spotted right where the Marines enter the flight deck from below to make it to their helos."

During actual combat ops, or training, twenty or so Marines were led by a sailor to one of the helos spotted along the port side of the flight deck. Once the sailor delivered the Marines to their conveyance ashore, he returned below decks. My concern was that in all the operations we had done to date, no sailor in our crew had ever led his line of Marines past a helo on that landing spot. Tail rotors were deadly weapons, and the guys coming out from below decks would have to pass close to the tail rotor on that extra spot.

"Boss," I said, "make sure—"

At that point there was an announcement of an emergency on the flight deck.

A young sailor had led his twenty Marines out from below decks. The helo on the extra spot had its rotors turning and the downdraft from the main rotors made him duck his head, and he walked right into the tail rotor.

A nineteen-year-old—I always think of him as a kid—man, Reggie. I see his face once a week. On a Tuesday, when I get his coffee mug out of the cabinet for what I call my *mourning cup of Joe*. Tuesday/Reggie's mug is emblazoned with a decal logo of the ship we crewed together, Reggie and me. And the mourning bit, of course I mourn for the man I killed, but I also mourn for man I should have been, but that man did not show up for work that day.

Okay, I think I told you about the sin above because I did not want to excavate one of my failure-to-prevent-a-suicide sins. I need to dig it out.

After I retired from the US Navy, I went to work for an aerospace company. During my last couple of years before my second retirement, I worked on a program to supply new airplanes to my old service. On the program with me was Missy Sadler. Ex US Army officer and expert in logistics. She managed the support end of our project. A tough lady. Don't get pissy with Missy. That was the word.

Anyway, after I retired-retired, we moved back to Jolene's hometown. There I wound up getting an invite to serve on the advisory board at the high school Jolene and I graduated from.

One evening I pulled into the high school parking lot with three minutes to spare before a meeting, when my cell rang. Caller ID proclaimed: Missy Sadler. *Why would she be calling me?*

"Missy," I said. "How are you?" said all bright and cheerful, you know?

"Nah so good, Notso." Her voice sure sounded not so good.

"What's wrong?"

"I … I jus wanned tawk wif you."

"Missy, are you drunk?"

She hung up. I looked at the phone, thought about dialing back. But she was drunk. I decided to call her in the morning. I was now three minutes late for my meeting.

Missy committed suicide that night.

So there's a Missy mug in my collection.

Since the other Mudgeon's confession, this Missy sin feels like a nest of termites in my Pinocchio soul.

And here I am, drafting Dispatches which presumed to tell other people how they needed to change. When who really needed to change more than anyone else on the whole blinking planet?

Me, myself, and I only. That's who.

I never was worthy of the task of drafting Mudgeon Dispatches. I just couldn't see it before.

The Mudgeon had harbored one sin. I had four. He carried the guilt for his sin. I felt like I carried seventy times four the amount of guilt he carried.

I will say, the Mudgeon's confession

spurred me to make my own confession of those four sins. To a priest.

My first sin happened fifty years ago. I built a cocoon around it. The same thing with next three. I wound up with quadruplet cocoons in my sin closet. The Mudgeons confession just busted those cocoons open. Only butterflies didn't crawl out. The ugliest wasps ever created crawled out. They had grasshopper faces, and they drooled tobacco juice as they chewed.

An ugly bug face was the face I saw on my soul.

So I am not worthy to draft Dispatches. I am not worthy to be a Mudgeon.

The Mudgeons evolved from crusty old poops, with a boatload of help from our HERmudgeons, into beings with beautiful souls.

Creed Two says we should "hang onto hope." I hope enough of your soulular beauty has rubbed off on me so that, when I stand before St. Pete, he won't give me a thumbs down. I hope he gives me a thumb-sideways signal. Cooking in Purgatory for eons may just fry away my waspy-ness and show there really was a butterfly buried within my soul.

Just one more thing. And it's not a tiny thing.

In digging out that cocoon, I discovered another sin. It is deep-seated animosity toward the generations younger than me, except for my children, grandchildren, and greatgrandchildren. And a handful, or two, of young people I had the privilege of getting to know well enough to see they had butterflies cocooned in their souls.

This animosity goes back to the Vietnam War days. Then, I became convinced the people (most of them young, and younger than I was at the time by five to ten years) protesting against our involvement in the Vietnam War weren't protesting the war so much as they protested against the United States of America. I thought they were wrong, and their *misguided protest* is what motivated me to stay in the service and to apply for flight training.

This animosity turned into prejudice, and I've come to see this prejudice as a major driver in my motivation to convince young people they need to change.

So, a second reason why I'm not worthy to continue as a Mudgeon.

But, I have enough in me to thank you, Mudgeons, and you young people, for helping me see why, what, where, how, and when I needed to change myself. Thank you.

So, I Gregory George Notso Normal do hereby resign from the Mudgeons.

Gregory Geohn

I, Jolene, think what happened is GG had typed his letter and then added "Gregory Ge" when he collapsed. When I pulled him off the keyboard, the laptop typed "ohn."

Yesterday I heard a rumor. Apparently, some people, after reading GG's letter think he was depressed and intentionally stopped taking his meds.

That is not true.

How do I know?

I know because GG told me so.

Yesterday, I went to visit his grave. I took one of his blood thinner pills with me and ground it into the dirt above him, and I asked him. He answered.

Sweetheart. I would never do anything to shorten my time on earth with you. Besides I have all these stinkin sins on my soul. Who the crap knows where I'll wind up! Why would I be in a hurry to get there?

I think that answers that question.

I dropped my hands into my lap. The laptop looked back at me as if asking, "Are you sure you're done?"

I blew my nose. I do that a lot these days. If my eyes aren't crying, my nose is.

I needed another cup of coffee and went to the kitchen to get one.

Back at the desk, I set the mug of hot stuff to the side, placed my fingers on the keyboard, and they typed.

Gregory George you sure aren't Normal. You ARE exceptional. Through the preceding Dispatches you set out a goal for us. Find a way to get along with each other better. Instead of You People and Us People, become We the people. Through study, you found behavior modifications to suggest to us, but you took each of those suggestions

and infused them into your soul. You,
by the transformation you worked into
your own soul, showed us how to be
what you called us to be. And man,
you are worthy as all get out.

I sat back in the chair and wondered what the
Board of Directors would think of my draft.

They'll love it.

"Are you sure?"

Of course, I'm sure.

He sounded sure. I picked up the coffee and took
a drink.

*See, Number twenty-one wasn't hard. The next one
hundred will be even easier.*

I snorted coffee out my nose and dropped the mug
in my lap. Thank You, God, it was warm and not hot.
It didn't waste any time, though, turning cold. And,
"Look at the white carpeting!"

If you mop it up fast, if won't stain. Too bad.

Then it sank in. "One hundred more Dispatches,
you said?"

*Yes. Of course, I am new at this seeing the future
business, but that's what it looks like to me.*

"Jesus, Mary, and Joseph!"

I'll be here to help.

"Then clean up the spill."

*Sorry. Union rules prevent me. But after you mop up
the mess, I'll show you something on the laptop.*

"Union rules, my foot!"

But I cleaned the mess and took the laptop to the kitchen table.

Go to documents.

"Uh—"

The cursor moved over a square smiley face in the lower left corner of the screen. A pop down list of items showed up. One was a folder labeled "Future Disp."

I opened the folder to a half a dozen Word documents. One of them was entitled "Black lives matter." I opened it. I skimmed through the first two pages. Among a number of other things, he'd written "there is an air of <u>only Black lives matter</u> in the movement. In later pages, he'd written about the number of white lives lost to gain a place where Black lives mattered. His point was that Black lives always mattered to a lot of whites, and that the real point was that all lives mattered.

Dear Lord! What will the Board of Directors think of this?

I closed the file and shut down the laptop. I had no more Mudgeon business left in me today.

I turned on the TV in the kitchen and called up HGTV. *Cooking or Home Remodeling?* As I flipped through channels, I thought that I should have been watching out for GG during the holidays when things got so hectic. I should have noticed he wasn't taking his pills.

But GG, you'd begun talking to me about deep and meaningful things. I'd been so hungry for that all through our fifty-nine years of marriage, I couldn't see beyond how wonderful it had suddenly become.

"Sorry, GG. But if I learned one thing from you, it's that I should not take this guilt and stuff it deep into the belly of my soul."

Ah. "Beat Bobby Flay." I laid the remote on the table.

How about "Gunsmoke?"

I frowned. Then my face smiled. "Yes, Dear."

I went downstairs and turned on channel 546. Festus was speaking Notso speak. I shook my head and returned to Bobby Flay. Win or lose Bobby spoke normal speak.

Five minutes after I sat, Bobby won.

I sighed, rose, and returned to the downstairs. I sat in the center of the sofa. GG always sat in the right corner.

"Don't get used to this. I am not watching "Gunsmoke" with you every day."

Shh! It's six minutes before the end. This is when the bad guy bites the dust.

Then the station cued up a commercial.

You did a good job on the dispatch.

"The draft is as much you as it is me."

That's because we are not welded at the hip. We are welded at the soul.

"You're still not taking a shower with me."

Ratsnot!

"Shhh! Marshal Dillon's back."

COPs' CREED

1. The world is going to hell in a handbasket and is hell-bent-for-election to get there.
2. There IS something we can do about it. Stop shouting and listen. Seek balance. Hang onto Hope.
3. Find one opportunity to forgive an annoying dweeb every day. Then go all the way to Love Thy Neighbor as Thyself.
4. COPs must complete the COP required reading list. COPs should always be on the lookout for other good books to read. In addition to reading books, COPs must learn to read themselves.
5. Number Three above does not apply if the dweeb is waving a gun in your face.
6. Self-delusion, the human autopilot, and a powerful instinct to band together are insidious beasts. Guard against them.
7. Before you tell others how to act, examine

your own behavior. Do not go easy on yourself.

8. The history of politics in America is one of continuous acrimony that threatened to, and once did, tear the country apart. With some measure of harmony in the political process, both sides stand to gain some of what they seek. And both sides will be better served if the union is preserved than if it tears itself apart.

9. There is a time for every purpose under heaven. Discerning when to support some of these purposes require continuous soul-searching. Do not expect it to be morally easy.

10. Our country never stopped being great. Appreciate that every day.

COPS' READING LISTS

Required Reading List

1. *The Ox-Bow Incident*, by Walter Van Tilburg Clark. Read the book or watch the movie. Doing both is best.
2. *Rules, A Short History of What We Live by*, by Lorraine Daston.
3. *The Age of Acrimony*, by Jon Grinspan.

Note: We encourage readers of our Dispatches to find their own books to read. We further encourage you to forward those titles to us COPs for inclusion on our Recommended Reading List. Such as the following:

Recommended Reading List

1. *To Rescue the Republic*, by Bret Baier with Catherine Whitney.

2. Frederick *Douglass, Prophet of Freedom*, by David W. Blight.
3. The Bible.
4. *The President's Club*, by Nancy Gibbs and Michael Duffy.
5. *The Rise and Fall of the Third Reich*, by William Shirer.

Note: The Mudgeons are considering adding *Tombstone* by Tom Clavin to one of the reading lists.